Unconditional Love Deadly Love
By
Rose Varela-Van Dyke

Dedication

For my mother and sister

Afterlife 1: an existence after death
Webster

Part One
The Good-bye
"You know the consequences."

ONE
The Catacombs

The catacombs of the afterlife are not very large—the size of an average coffin. The soul always accommodates its surroundings, while good emotions never seem to have enough space. The boundless space of heaven is not enough room for loving emotions. In comparison, the coffin size passage is much too large for hateful sentiments.

In the beginning, it is not blissful. Leaving the body and allowing the soul to drift out into the catacomb is not at all heavenly.

For the good soul, drifting out is as good as it gets. For the good soul, lingering in the catacomb with the guide is not unusual for a short period.

For the bad soul, ripping out is as good as it gets. For the sinful soul, it never gets better. The catacomb, unable to filter out a lifetime of badness, eventually rips the soul out of the frail body, and it is over.

The catacomb becomes the oblivion crypt from bad to evil in a heaven minute. The journey ends. It is that simple and that complicated in the catacombs of the afterlife.

Now and then, a rare incident occurs—read on.

***

Clayton's fading body stood in the middle of the brilliant white empty catacomb. Clayton stared down into nothingness wild with grief, thinking, what happened? Jason. The name brought tears to his eyes, my son, gone—even my memories of his existence soon gone for all eternity. Slowly moving his gaze up, an insane idea came to him. Shall I warn others? Shall I tell them of the catacombs of the afterlife?

Alma gently took his hand, bringing Clayton out of his crazy thoughts. She softly muttered, "Clayton, we must cross back. Our job here finished. We have swept all the bad energies. Let's not risk bringing them back. No one is immune on this side. We are weak right now. Cleansing a room of bad emotions drains the soul to dangerous levels of confusion and mistrust. These highly potent emotions will risk our return. We are in the same jeopardy that befell our son, Andrea, and Sage. It is painful. Sad they had to perish." Her voice started to tremble.

The weakened condition they were in and trying to maintain positive energy overwhelmed and frightened Alma. The thought of what could happen to them—chilling.

"Clayton, we must go. Our souls cannot absorb more negative thoughts."

Annoyed by Alma's demeanor, Clayton scorned, "Sad? How can you be so casual? Sad was when Jason lost his turtle." That memory brought a smile to Clayton. He paused for a moment, chuckled gently, then said, "Remember, Sweetheart? We were at the summer cabin, Jason, seven years old at the time. He wanted to take his turtle for a swim in Lake Michigan. We suggested he have a turtle race instead of a turtle swim. Jason darted outside with the turtle in hand. We didn't give much thought to the incident. A few minutes later, Jason came running into the cabin, dripping wet, sand all over him. Big tears streaming down his face, he bawled, "My turtle swam away."

Clayton's reminiscence of that time also provoked laughter in Alma. He paused for a moment realizing again all of Jason's memories would soon be gone. "That was sad, Alma; this is incorrigible grief."

3

Clayton's ghostly body fell to its knees, trying to maintain control. Quivering, he said, "We should be overjoyed now. The transition should be complete; all of us crossing over sharing in eternal peace and love."

Alma calmly interrupted, "I know Clayton. We haven't much time. You must compose yourself. We cannot cross back with these thoughts. Our souls must have peace and love."

The bright white room less brilliant, scarcely noticeable to Clayton, Alma felt the negative energy, death. They were both on the threshold of true death.

His physical body weary, Clayton stood. Straining to maintain control, he firmly said, "Alma. Cross back without me. I need a few minutes to myself. I'll cross back shortly."

Hesitant but trustworthy of her husband, Alma said, "All right, Clayton. You know the consequences."

The two shadowy figures took advantage of the brief illusion of touch allowed in the catacomb. Wearily, strolling hand in hand, they searched for the doorway.

Alma proudly stated, "We had a great life." She softly stroked his ghostlike chest then lovingly caressed his face. "Eternity is better, Clayton."

Hugging affectionately, they turned the room brilliant white again. "Here is the spot to cross back, feel the positive energies," Alma said.

They looked deeply into each other's phantom eyes. Softly as a butterfly alights on a flower, they kissed.

In this weakened state, both needed to touch the energetic spot. In a heavenly flash, the blinding, glorious entrance opened. Alma stepped across. Not looking back, she softly echoed, "You know the consequences."

Her weary physical body vanished. She was now pure loving energy, a glowing soul melding with other eternal loving souls—an easy transformation when the cross over is allowed.

Clayton watched Alma leave her body and transform into good energy. It mesmerized him. The aperture opened and closed as quickly as a photographer's camera clicks, trying to capture a feeding hummingbird's

4

eating frenzy. The vanishing entrance startled Clayton; this was the first time he saw it disappear. The loneliness he felt shocked him. He knew the peace that existed on the other side of the catacomb portal. Why had he done this?

Exposure to the brilliant loving light rejuvenated Clayton like the sun heals the physical body. The body he once knew returned.

Clayton touched his physical illusion, knowing full well it was an illusion. His soul remembered touch and memories in the earthly body—memories he should not probe but did.

He touched his face. What do I look like? Do I still have mothers' eyes and chin? He vaguely remembered wrinkles appearing. His face didn't feel like it had wrinkles. What are wrinkles supposed to feel like? He had a full head of hair. Is it still grey? It started turning grey in his twenties. By the time he turned thirty, his hair was a beautiful silvery white. 'You're just starting to look distinguished,' Remembering Alma's words brought a smile. Yes, Alma, we did have a great life. Even in eternity, our souls overlap.

He slowly walked around the catacomb striving for inner peace as good energy still abound.

Clayton thought Alma is right; I must regain my inner peace. I must.

His thoughts were interrupted by a form beginning to appear in the middle of the room. He had witnessed this before—a soul emerging from the physical world. And this had to be an infant soul. Baby souls never enter a catacomb alone, nor good-byes needed for a peaceful cross-over.

Awaiting the emergence of the baby, Clayton watched the spot readily. The little body was becoming more and more visible, like a baby bird pecking its way out of the shell.

Finally, the cross over complete, a sudden warm wind completed the cross over. This innocent little soul becomes an instant angel.

Clayton bent over the little crying form. He touched the soft spot evoking, "Behold peace and joy," As he merrily smiled at the baby.

The baby opened his eyes and smiled as if he knew he was safe. Indeed he was.

"That's all precious little angel; the earthly pain is gone forever."

Cradling the baby in his arms brought back recollections of happy times. Memories of Jason and his granddaughter, Sage.

The energy of the guiltless soul gave Clayton extra time in the catacomb. The time he needed to sort things out, to ponder what had happened.

Clayton's body, a strong illusion now, sat comfortably on the floor. Being protective of the child, he gently said, "Little angel, I want to tell you of an incident. Maybe this way, I'll find my peace."

He gently stroked the baby's face. Clayton listened to the innocent coos, his memories now becoming more vivid. Clayton knew he had to stay longer. The child gave him strength allowing him to go on with his quest.

Clayton softly said, "It's about my son and his family.

This nightmare started when my granddaughter Sage died and her mother, Andrea, divulged to me what she allowed to happen."

Clayton stared at the baby and nothing. The innocent coos peacefully took him to contemplations of his family.

TWO
Jason

Jason raced to the hospital as soon as he got the call about his daughter. Trance-like, Rudy sat on the hospital bench, unaware of people entering and exiting the waiting room.

"Rudy. What's going on? Where is Sage?"

Rudy heard a familiar voice, and his expressionless face looked up to see Jason approaching.

In a quivering voice, Rudy spurted out, "Dad." Darting toward Jason and hugging him.

Composed, Jason stated, "I got here as fast as I could. I received a call from the hospital. They said something happened to my daughter. They wouldn't tell me anything else. What's going on?"

Sobbing, "They took her. She's somewhere in an emergency room," Rudy managed to say.

"What happened?" Jason asked impatiently.

Trying to hold back the tears, Rudy blubbered, "We were getting ready for tonight or last night? I can't remember. I had to write a short speech, not paying much attention to anything else. I vaguely heard Sage exclaim she was going to the laundry room. Something she had to wear. I don't remember what. Why couldn't she find something else to wear? Why did this happen? We had everything going for us."

Starting to get annoyed, Jason calmly asked again, "What happened?"

"I don't know. I finished my speech, went to take a shower. As I combed my hair, I realized Sage was not around. I called her several times didn't hear a response. That was unusual. Sage always answered when I called her. I finished my hair and got dressed."

Rudy wiped the uncontrollable tears with his arm, cleared his throat.

"I started looking for her. I didn't think she would still be in the laundry room, so I didn't look there. I looked everywhere, even in parts of the house that were off-limits," He sobbed.

Rudy stopped, unable to go on.

Patiently waiting for Rudy to calm down, Jason noticed a small woman with unnatural red-orange hair strolling toward them. A black cord belt separated her black outfit into a flowing floor-length skirt. He had never met Rudy's mother in person, but Sage had described her impeccably. He knew it was Julia and he started to feel uneasy. The closer she came, the more uneasy Jason felt.

"Rudy, my son, come hug your mother."

At the same time, she takes a small covered jar out of her large black leather handbag and quickly unscrewed the lid, she said, "Drink this Baby, it will calm you."

Without hesitation, Rudy took the jar. He drank the gelatinous concoction as if it were nutritious nectar.

As she watched her son drink, Ms. Julia extended her arm in a robot-like fashion toward Jason, blandly asking, "How are you, Mister Jason?"

Jason cautiously clasped her hand for a second. He knew her smile was fake, and his patience, running short.

He responded, "I'm numb. Rudy is trying to explain what happened to my daughter."

"Son. What happened? Where is Sage?" Ms. Julia asked in a controlled hypnotic voice.

Hiccupping, Rudy said. "After looking everywhere, even outside, I decided to look in the laundry room. Opening the door, I see her sprawled

8

on the floor. It appeared as if she had been trying to get to the door. I ran toward her motionless body. I jiggled her, shouted her name—nothing. For a split second, I became panic-stricken. I didn't know what to do. I ran to the phone, dialed nine-one-one." Rudy sighed, wiping his nose on his sleeve.

"Now here we are—waiting. I think I've been waiting for about an hour. I don't know. I still don't know about her condition. They took her, and no one has been back."

Ms. Julia had walked behind her son and was sounding low muffled chants. She dangled a little red canvas bag in her right hand at times, caressing Rudy's body with the small red bag. And her left hand held the charm around her neck. She placed the charm on the back of Rudy's neck. The ritual, coupled with the tea, soothed the inner soul. Oblivious to the surroundings, she continued the practice until she felt her son was calm. She would know when to stop.

Jason exploded, "What the hell are you doing?"

"My special chants and the tea will soothe his inner soul."

"Stop this crap, get out of here."

"I'll stop when I know my son's life forces are back in balance."

Jason seethed, "Go home and take your maricon with you. As far as I'm concerned, your son killed my daughter. I never approved of them living together. The day my daughter met Rudy was the day she died."

Sounding like a howling wolf, Rudy sobbed. Ms. Julia hugged him. She put the red pouch in his pocket while fishing for something in her bag.

"Dad. How can you say that? Sage adored me I."

"Don't call me Dad, you son-of-a-bitch. Leave. You have no place here. I will decide what will happen to my daughter. Her fate is in my hands. You've done enough damage."

Ms. Julia pulled out a little black satin bag from her pocket and started waving it at Jason, chanting wildly. She appeared to be in a trance; her stare pierced through Jason. Suddenly her eyes disappeared into her sockets, leaving only little white eyeballs.

Jason yelled, "You bitch. Get that crap out of my face." He reached for the bag. He wanted to snatch it so he could stomp it. So he could kill it.

9

Maybe by killing the bag, his pain would ease. He had never felt such rage.

Protecting her sacred bag, Ms. Julia sternly said, "Mister Jason, you don't know my power. I knew a year ago of your daughter's death. In the cosmos, a year is but a minute. I didn't know the exact day, but I knew it would be soon."

Astonished, Rudy stared at his mother, saying, "You never told me." His red eyes glared at his mother.

"Son. No one can do anything. When the time comes to leave the physical body, no one should interfere. That would be toying with the demons. For you, son, I gave Sage a charm. I instructed her on wearing it for her protection. The charm may have given her a little more time."

Ms. Julia tenderly caressed Rudy's face, kissed him gently on the forehead, hugged his head toward her bosom.

"We will never know the power of the charm. I took a chance to toy with the demons of death, a road not to be traveled for the unprepared. I interfered for you, my son. Sage has gone to another plane. She is no longer of this world."

Jason roared, "I don't believe in your mumbo jumbo. You and Rudy had Sage convinced about this stupid crap. Rudy turned my beautiful innocent girl into a zombie. It'll take more than your voodoo to shut me up. Now take your so-called son and LEAVE."

Ms. Julia started her protective chant as she took hold of her tormented son.

Rudy's cries almost convinced Jason that he was sincere. The thought lasted only a millisecond. Thinking of his precious daughter alone, somewhere in the ER made it a ridiculous idea. Jason watched as Rudy and Ms. Julia departed the hospital.

Sitting in solitude, not knowing about his daughter, the fiasco with Ms. Julia and Rudy, Jason tried to make sense of what had happened.

"Jason." A voice brought him back to reality.

Drained of emotions, Jason quickly answered, "Yes."

"Hi. I am Doctor Barelas. Your daughter is in the ICU. We managed to get a heartbeat."

"May I see her?" At that moment, Jason did not care about anything else;

10

he just had to see his daughter.

"Come with me." The Doctor said in a professionally detached voice.

The walk to her room seemed endless. As they entered the room, Jason saw monitors and tubes trailing everywhere. He heard steady beeping sounds but, not prepared for this: A pale motionless little girl fastened to lines surrounded by flashing monitors. He immediately ran toward her, took her frail hand, and gently massaged it.

"Jason, your daughter is in a coma. She will die if we remove the life support systems."

"Are you sure? If there is a slight chance, a glimmer of hope, I won't take her off life support."

"Nothing is absolute. In the likelihood your daughter survives, she will be in a comatose state," The doctor said, still detached from any emotion.

Those words pierced Jason's heart.

"What happened to her? I still don't know the cause of this infernal nightmare."

Doctor Barelas softened his tone, saying, "Your daughter had a high concentration of carboxyhemoglobin, which caused carbon monoxide poisoning."

"Carbon monoxide poisoning? My beautiful Sage is gone because of something so inane? How can this be God? Take me! She had so much to live for, so much energy. She's too young to die. Take me." Jason could not hold back the tears.

Jason felt so alone. The room began to spin. He saw blurred objects, bright lights but felt no hope for Sage nor himself.

Doctor Barelas placed his hand on Jason's shoulder, softly said, "Jason. I know this isn't easy. However, you must decide if you want to keep her on life support."

Jason was not in the room. He felt the doctor touch his shoulder, but his thoughts were not in the room. He saw Sage laughing and enjoying life. She should be enjoying life.

An extra loud beep brought him back to the room.

The doctor said, "It's a warning sound; a fresh IV bag is going to be needed soon."

"Doctor, I can't decide now. I see her sleeping so innocently. Like when she was a baby. So innocent. How can I destroy her?"

The doctor listened to Jason's rambling, "Next month, January 13[th;] she would've been twenty-one years old. I wanted Sage to have a huge birthday party; she didn't want one. She said, 'Daddy, it's a Friday. Friday the 13th,' I suggested celebrating Saturday. She said, 'Daddy, I would still know it's Friday.' I laughed. So we decided no big celebration—just us and Rudy. I did not like him. Sage said, 'Give him a chance, Daddy. Look at him through my eyes. You'll love him too.'

Jason paused.

"Thanks for listening, Doctor. How long do I have to make this decision?"

"I know this is difficult, Jason, but you should know. The longer she stays on life support, the worse it will be. Not only will this be financially draining, emotionally, this will also be arduous. Imagine seeing your beautiful daughter at eighty pounds, losing her teeth and in a fetal position. She would be a living corpse."

"Stop. Doctor, stop!" Jason whispered.

Always a man of composure, except when it involved Sage.

"I'll give you my answer tomorrow." Jason managed to say.

"Very well, but remember what I said. This situation," motioning at Sage's almost lifeless body, "will not get better."

The Doctor left the room, leaving Jason staring at his daughter.

Jason softly spoke, telling Sage, "I knew Rudy was no good for you." He gently combed her dull, tangled hair with his fingers. He took her rigid hand, gently caressed it.

He found the strength to continue the one-sided conversation.

"You can't leave me yet, Sweet Basil. You haven't lived long enough. You have so much to experience. I was looking forward to your long-distance calls once you became a flight attendant. Your traveling career was going to be exciting. We had it all planned. I would guess your first three assignments, three wrongs, and I would buy you any car you wanted. Great plan, huh?"

Jason took a hairbrush from the bedside table. He started brushing her hair, thinking Sage would never leave the house with messy hair.

"That's better. I fixed your hair, Sweetheart. You know I'm always here for you." Jason quietly stared, waiting to hear Sage say, 'Da-a-a-d,' his mind distinctively heard her childish whine.

"I had so much left to tell you. I never found the time to tell you about your grandparents, Alma and Clayton. They were wonderful. Sure, you saw pictures, but to know them through my memories, I should have told you long ago. I never explained how they died. You were too young. It was difficult for me to talk about it. As you got older, I should have told you about them. But I also didn't want you to forget your mom; her memory needed engraving in your mind. She loved you so much."

Jason pressed his eyes shut, trying to lubricate them. His salty tears had dried them out. Ironically, the eye irritation kept him from going numb.

"Your grandparents died in a car accident. They were driving from Indiana to celebrate your first Christmas. They had to be with you no matter what. You were their only grandchild. On their way here, the weather abruptly turned dastardly cold and frigid. Dad lost control of the car on a patch of black ice. The vehicle went through a guardrail plummeting sixty feet down. They both died instantly.

When the police called about the accident, your mother and I were putting up the Christmas tree. We were going to decorate it once they arrived. Our joyous moment turned tragic."

Jason stopped. His emotions so high, his grief beyond control. He stood there, motionless. He stared at his pale daughter, hoped to see movement— a response of any kind. Nothing happened. He looked at the machines. Numbers and lights flickering, a steady pumping sound but no life sounds. No laughter, no joy, no tears.

Jason took a deep breath, tenderly kissed Sage's parched lips, and whispered, "I'll see you tomorrow."

Jason tucked her in, safe in the strange surroundings. He convinced himself Sage would be okay. Blindly grabbing the door handle, he turned to stare at Sage. Still, no movement. He gently opened the door and silently

13

left the room.

Jason departed with an emptiness in his heart and loneliness that reached the depths of his soul.

THREE
Sage

Sluggishly opening her dull, lifeless green eyes, Sage thought, why didn't Rudy wake me up? Wait till I see him. She wiped the sleep from her eyes, realizing it wasn't so bad after all. Explaining his actions to herself, he knew I was exhausted. Rudy is just being thoughtful.

Sage couldn't remember what had made her so tired. She and Rudy were supposed to go out to dinner, then party until dawn celebrating their graduations. Talking to herself, she said, "I should be getting ready. I don't even know what I'm wearing."

Sage stretched her long slender arms as far as she could reach, then sat up. She ran her fingers through her shoulder-length ebony hair. Shaking and fluffing it at the same time. In a Hungarian accent, gruffly said, "Beautiful dahling."

Smiling and somewhat more alert thought, why is the house so quiet? Talking to the emptiness, "Rudy, are you there?" Sage lazily got out of bed. She started walking around the house, talking to herself, "I guess he's not here. Why didn't he leave me a note? I'm supposed to speculate when he's coming back? I hate when he does this," She slowly fumed.

In the silence of her thoughts, I better not think about it, or I'll get upset. Rudy will be home soon. I need to get ready.

Sage yawned and slowly entered the bathroom. She looked in the mirror, not believing her reflection. "Omigod, what happened to me? No wonder Rudy let me sleep longer."

Her beautiful silky smooth olive-colored skin appeared dry and pallid. Her big gorgeous green eyes were swimming in an ocean of red. Her black hair the worst she had ever seen; it had no luster, no sheen of any kind.

"Yuk! I had a long nap. I should have rosy cheeks and sparkling eyes." She pinched her cheeks and palpitated her eyelids. Nothing happened. The mirror image still looked sickly. Opening her mouth, she stuck out her tongue. It had a slight blackish appearance.

"Thath nathy!"

Sage thought, an invigorating hot shower, some make-up, I'll be stunning again.

Talking to the reflection, "I better get started; it's going to take longer than I thought, and I still don't know what I'm going to wear."

The sound of the doorbell brought her out of her thoughts. She grumbled out loud, "Great. Just what I need. Company. I better see who it is; with two celebrations tonight, anything can happen."

Sage hastily slipped into her teal blue terry cloth robe, and white fuzzy slippers trotted downstairs to the entrance. Angrily thinking, where's Rudy? He should be doing this.

Opening the door, she had to shield her eyes from the bright light. The brightness made it impossible to see, prompting her to ask, "Who's there?"

"Hi, Sage, it's mother." A resounding voice said.

"Mom? What are you doing here?"

"Isn't that a lovely greeting for your mother?" Andrea chuckled.

"I didn't mean it that way, Mom."

Andrea entered hugged Sage as never before. The brightness subdued as Andrea could not maintain the physical body very long in this cross-over world, the comatose state of life and death. It was a difficult place for the soul to endure. Unable to detach from the physical body, the

soul fights unmercifully to enter the catacombs of the afterlife peacefully. Man-made life maintains the physical body but not the soul.

"Mother, I'm so busy right now. It seems I don't even know who I am. Come in, come in. I'm getting ready to take a shower. I don't know why I'm a nervous wreck. It isn't supposed to be this hectic. I've overslept, and,"

16

Andrea softly interrupted, "Calm down. I am here to help make your soul

serene until the good-byes are said."

Oblivious to her mother's words, Sage continued, "Oh mother, look at my hair. My complexion is the worst; all I need is a zit. Of all nights, and I still don't know what I'm wearing." Sage shouted, oblivious to her mother's comforting words.

Andrea softly touched Sage's shoulder. Continuing in her soothing tone, Andrea said, "None of this matters if you are at peace with yourself. You must be at peace with yourself before the good-byes are said. Peace allows for an easier transition."

"Mother, this is a fabulous time in my life; I want to look spectacular as all my friends are going to be at the party. And I have to stop by Daddy's. He has to see me spectacular otherwise, he'll think something is wrong."

"I know you do. It will be wonderful. You are very confused right now. I've waited so long for you. I couldn't wait anymore. I had to come and see you. Help you attain some harmony until the good-byes. This moment will help make you peaceful. I'll see you again, hopefully very soon. Next time I will be joined by your Grandma Jenny and Auntie Rita."

Andrea's tranquility finally helped Sage sustain some harmony.

Reminiscing aloud, Sage said, "I haven't seen Grandma or Auntie in a long time. It'll be great seeing them. I've missed Grandmother's peppermint candy. She always had some in her pockets. Do you suppose she'll have a piece?"

Andrea tenderly stroked her daughter's pale face saying, "Be patient. It will be wonderful. I must leave now."

Without saying another word, Andrea tightly hugged her daughter and departed.

The departure left Sage calm and warm, a warmth she had not felt in a long time.

Closing the door, Sage smiled, "I'm glad mom was here; I needed her encouragement. I can't wait to tell Rudy about her visit, and Grandmother and Aunt Rita will visit soon. Rudy will like them. I know it. Though, I seem to remember something about them? Grandma, Aunt Rita, left on a journey. They left, and—and mother joined them. It must be the—"

Sage's thoughts abruptly went blank. Confused thoughts swirled through
her mind: the calmness, the warmth gone.

"What's happening to me? I can't remember anything."

She looked at her hands. They were dry and scaly. Her fingernails were slightly purple, "My hands!"

Sage stared at her withered arms; they moved on their own, reached for her hair—straw. The hands touched straw, not her beautiful silky hair. Then exhaustion overtook her. She did not have the energy to worry about anything. Nothing mattered. She wanted to sleep, find peace, as her mother had said. She slowly walked to the bed.

"I'm so tired."

Her eyelids slowly closed, bringing Sage into a deep involuntary sleep.

FOUR
Andrea

Andrea brought in the last of the bags. Her kitchen became cluttered with bags of groceries and party decorations. She could not wait to get started; Jason would be home in about two hours. She had to set the mood for her delightful update. She was pregnant. They decided the news had to be face to face instead of a phone call. Their love too perfect for just voices on a line.

They had put off having a baby, Andrea, at thirty-eight, didn't think it now possible. They had a thriving restaurant and food consulting business. They loved each other implicitly, yet something was still missing. A void existed—they realized a baby. Three months ago, they had agreed it was time to get pregnant.

Andrea put her purse and keys on top of the desk near the kitchen, her favorite room. The kitchen invariably evoked warmth and love. She created delicious foods here with aromas to drive the entire being scrumptiously mad. Her culinary creativity bubbled in this kitchen.

Knowing she had to cheat time, Andrea had stopped at the Gourmet Eatery to pick up some prepared food. In a pinch, the Eatery was the best. On busy days, she recommended the Eatery to some clients.

She never understood why people waited until the last minute to order food. Andrea intuitively knew when people didn't know anything about food preparation because she always talked them into ordering chicken. Poultry dishes were excellent. Quick, easy, and profitable

Especially during the holidays, they could get away with charging outrageous prices for chicken.

At the Eatery, she purchased the salmon, blueberry mousse, and a bottle of fumé blanc. The couscous, salad, lemon sauce, and vinegarette were a snap to make.

After leaving the Eatery, she stopped at the florist and bought a bouquet of babies' breath. A pair of gaudy stork candles grabbed her attention. She had to buy them.

Trying to bring some order into her kitchen, she glanced at the clock, three-fifteen, time to hustle. The evening would be flawless.

She brought out a small crystal bowl. It was perfect for her centerpiece of babies' breath. She added dainty pink and blue silk ribbons. Perfect.

The dining room would be too formal for the beautiful evening planned. Instead, Andrea walked to the breakfast nook, set the perfect centerpiece on the table. Their table.

The old grungy table they'd found at a secondhand store. After having it refinished, an elegant, warm maple table surfaced. The wood craftsman remarked how beautifully the maple wood had revitalized. He built two matching maple chairs, charging them half price. It was a pleasure to work on such beautiful old wood, meant to be in their happy kitchen.

Next, she took the stork candles from the white paper bag and placed one on either side of the centerpiece. The gaudy candles became beautiful next to the baby's breath, or maybe the delicate ribbons made them lovely. Whatever made them stunning, Andrea had known they would be perfect.

The next bag contained two linen placemats and napkins: one placemat pink, the other blue, likewise, the napkins. Andrea set one place with the pink mat and the other with the blue, vice versa with the napkins.

She then strolled to the china cabinet in the dining room and took two Spode china settings and two crystal wine glasses. Returning to the breakfast nook, she arranged the table settings.

Another bag revealed a blue infant receiving blanket. Andrea carefully opened the package took out the wrap. Touching the fuzzy blue cloth gave her a warm feeling. Yes, it was time to get pregnant. Delicately unfolding

the baby blanket on the kitchen counter, she began smoothing and stretching
it flat with the palm of her hands. She lifted one corner, folding it diagonally to the opposite corner, forming a triangle.

Positioning the wine bottle on the triangle, Andrea wrapped it in the blanket. She took the same blue and pink silk ribbon she had used on the centerpiece and tied it securely around the bottleneck, fanning the tips of the triangular corners.

"Voilà! Perfect. I think Jason will get the hint." Andrea whispered at the bottle.

She placed the adorned bottle in the vertical wine holder, smiled with joy at her achievements. She moved back to the kitchen area.

Popping open the food container, Andrea carefully removed the pink salmon, placing it on a china platter. She snipped some lavender from her garden window, rinsed it, then gently patted it dry, placing two sprigs on either side of the platter.

Placing a blue crystal bowl on the counter, she gently tore the rinsed baby bib lettuce, dropped it loosely into the bowl. She quickly rough chopped a medium purple Bermuda onion, two juicy Italian plum tomatoes, and four baby carrots. Gently scrubbed six baby mushrooms tossing all the vegetables lightly in a separate bowl. Set the mixed vegetables aside. She started making the croutons.

Andrea cubed two slices of whole wheat bread and threw the pieces in a veraciously hot oiled skillet. Immediately the bread sizzled. She sprinkled some poultry seasoning while shaking the skillet. The bread pieces tumbled around, became golden brown. Carefully poured the cubes onto a sheet pan and placed the pan in a warm oven. In a few minutes, the day-old bread pieces would become perfect croutons.

In the meantime, Andrea sprinkled the vegetables on top of the baby bib lettuce. The salad, done.

She took the olive oil, Andrea poured enough oil into a bowl for about two servings, adding a generous pinch of her unique herb blend. She slowly poured the raspberry vinegar, whisked, and poured. Whisking and pouring,

Andrea would know when to stop. The glistening bubbly liquid sufficiently mixed, she tasted for tartness—perfect. She emptied the vinegarette into a
serving dish—done.

Andrea took out the croutons, scooping the pieces onto a paper towel, then finely grated Parmesan cheese over the bread cubes. She grasped the four corners, gently shook the towel, emptied the pieces into a serving dish. The croutons—done.

Andrea quickly made the couscous and placed it in a serving dish. Done.

The meal, almost complete, Andrea gently opened the box containing the blueberry mousse. Delicately, she filled two silver goblets with the cloudlike dessert, storing them in the refrigerator. Perfect.

Stepping back, Andrea looked at the table—the cozy corner, the whimsical decorations, and a great menu would set the mood for the miraculous announcement.

Glancing at the clock, Andrea had time for one last surprise before Jason arrived.

She hurried to the bedroom with the final bag, slowly opened it. Removing an article wrapped in white tissue, carefully spread the tissue as if it would disclose a delicate orchid. She stared at the maternity top for a moment. Caressing the top, she brought it close to her body, hugged it, and smiled in ecstasy.

A voice called, ending her rapture—Jason. Andrea quickly took off her blouse and put on the yellow maternity top. She turned around and looked in the mirror. Big, bold black letters spelled BABY underneath the word, an arrow pointing down. She smiled and rubbed her flat tummy.

Jason's voice was getting closer; Andrea swiftly grabbed a smock
and put it on; just as she buttoned the last button, in walked Jason.
"Sweetheart." He said.

Briskly walked over to her and kissed her gently. "What happened? Are we pregnant? I've been excited and anxious all day. Please, tell me before I go, mad."

Andrea coyishly kissed him gently on the lips, said, "Close your eyes, and follow me."

Without hesitation, Jason closed his eyes as Andrea escorted him to the breakfast nook. Bantering, Jason said, "I think we're in the kitchen. The aroma is scrumptious. I must see what's generating those fabulous scents."

"Don't you dare, stand right here and don't open your eyes."

She quickly went to her place, removed the smock, threw it over her left shoulder. She lit the stork candles, aligned her top, making sure the arrow was perfect—at last ready.

"Okay, open your eyes."

Jason did as instructed. "Yahoo! We're pregnant." He rushed toward Andrea, gently hugged and kissed her.

"I won't break. Where are those passionate kisses I love so much?"

He embraced Andrea, and they kissed passionately.

Jason brought out the chair, helped Andrea sit, asking, "Are you comfortable?"

Andrea giggled, being lightheartedly wonderful, said, "I'm fine. Thanks."

He took the bottle of fumé blanc and poured some wine into each of their crystal glasses. Gracefully took his drink, saying, "A toast. May our future be as extraordinarily divine as our past." They clinked their glasses and savored the wine.

Jason went back to his chair, placing the napkin on his lap. He began to serve the salad saying, "Everything looks delicious. I haven't eaten all day."

He suddenly stopped and started laughing. The laugh turned to a smile.

"Where did you find those candles? They are quite, uh, what word would describe them?"

He paused, looked at them closer, then said, "Hmm. Charming, in a tawdry sort of way."

They both laughed. The evening went just as Andrea had planned, perfect. So perfect.

Eight and half months later, December 20, 1975, Andrea had stopped going to the restaurant but still consulting from home. Until now, she had a good pregnancy. The usual morning sickness only lasted a month. She didn't have many cravings, the midnight ice cream, the two a.m. spaghetti, not too many cravings. When she did, she made a small comment, and Jason would get it for her no matter the hour nor the desire.

Jason doted on Andrea, and he announced he, too, would stay home. Chef Rafael could handle everything.

Jason brought Andrea breakfast in bed and would get her bath ready.

Andrea loved baths. Especially now, the soothing bath suited her well to tolerate the dry, stretched skin. Jason helped her into the tub and became upset if she didn't call him to help her get out of the tub. His sulkiness would not last long. He gently toweled her body. He put his ear on her large tummy say, "I can hear her. It has to be a girl." Then in a high-pitched voice, he would say, "I'm almost ready, daddy." Confirm, "Yeah, it's a girl." Jason guided Andrea to the bedroom, delicately massage her legs and feet with
lotion, and rub body oil on her tummy.

The cold, dry winter months always instilled havoc on Andrea's skin, but it was worse this year. It had gotten so unbearable; she had to mention it to her Doctor on the last visit. The Doctor gave Andrea a prescription cream for dry skin to use as needed.

Andrea's appointments were now weekly.

A few other inconveniences Andrea did not tell Jason about, her dizzy spells. Nor did she mention the vomiting—just little annoyances. The birth of their precious baby would be here soon. These annoyances will be gone and forgotten, a small price to pay for a lifetime of joy.

Arriving at the Doctor's office, the always perky receptionist, Lauren, greeted Jason and Andrea. "Hi, Mr. and Mrs. Perkins, you're early. Good to see you. I've been working on your hospitalization packet. You have many forms to sign, Mrs. Perkins, but once we've finalized the package, I'll send it all to Hope Hospital. Then they'll just be waiting for your arrival."

Andrea and Jason smiled at each other. They could not wait to start their family.

Jason helped Andrea with her coat and scarf. She sat as he placed them on the coat hook. Jason removed her boots, replaced them with a pair of low flat black shoes.

"Thanks, Hun. That's much better." Sitting next to her, gently gave her a quick kiss.

The receptionist walked toward them with a clipboard in hand. "Here's the packet. All are required prior to your admittance. Insurance, liability next of kin, emergency procedures, all routine. Sign everywhere you see an X."

Handing the packet to Andrea, Lauren then took out two pens from her pocket. "Take your pick."

Andrea looked. One hot pink, the other vibrant yellow. Smiling, Andrea said, "Pink, of course."

Lauren giggled, handed her the pink pen. Andrea proceeded to read and sign the stack of forms.

The Doctor's office had a corner of the room, a child's paradise; games, books, a small sofa, and a child-size table with chairs. Cartoon characters decorated the walls with bird mobiles hung from the ceiling. They fluttered their wings mysteriously.

The tranquility of the cluttered corner maintained by soothing music, interchanged with ocean sounds, the sound of incoming tides brought illusions of a tranquil beach. The only thing missing was the smell of suntan lotion. The little corner mesmerized Jason. He couldn't wait to be in that cluttered corner with his little girl. The music program switched, bringing Jason out of his daydream.

Jason had insisted on driving. The weather horrible, with snow and patchy ice throughout the city. The drive was usually twenty minutes on this day, an hour. Andrea suggested she cancel the appointment. Jason adamantly disagreed. He felt something was not right.

"Mrs. Perkins." The clinical voice and unfamiliar.

"Yes," Andrea responded. As she made her way to the door, she asked Lauren, "Where is Holly?"

"She couldn't make it in. She lives in Joliet. Cindy subs on occasion to assist."

Glancing at the chart, Cindy said, "Please follow me to room three."

Andrea followed, knowing the routine all too well by now. Different nurse same routine. Cindy looked around the room, making sure everythingwas in order.

"Please put this on." Handing Andrea a hospital gown. "The doctor will be right in."

Andrea did as instructed. She sat on the examination table, waiting for the Doctor. Sitting on a cold plastic table covered with butcher paper with nothing on always made the wait a little scary. The skimpy hospital gown gave no protection.

Andrea heard a knock, then the door opened.

"Hi, Mrs. Perkins. How are you feeling? Terrible day to be out. I've had a lot of cancellations. I'm surprised you made it."

"I know. It took us an hour to get here. Jason drove. He insisted on keeping the appointment. I'm glad he drove; otherwise, I might have turned back and canceled too."

As she listened, Doctor Tobias took Andrea's blood pressure. Routinely jotted down the results in the chart and just as routinely said, "Legs up." Andrea slid around on the table like a roly-poly top and placed her socked feet on the stir ups.

"I suppose now is a good time to tell you, Doctor. I haven't been feeling well. I've been throwing up, and I get dizzy when I stand too long."

In a calm voice, Doctor Tobias asked, "Was it something you ate? How often have you been vomiting? What about this dizziness?"

"The vomiting started about two weeks ago—the dizziness about a month ago. I hadn't mentioned the dizziness because I thought I'd get over it soon, a little annoyance associated with pregnancy."

Doctor Tobias said, "That very well may be Andrea, but you should have mentioned this. Would I tell you how to bake a souffle?"

"I know I should have said something, but now what?"

Doctor Tobias automatically performed a stethoscopy, listening through the protruding tummy. As she listened, she said, "To be on the safe side, let's do some blood test." She jotted some notes on the chart then continued, "The holiday season is almost here. We will be closed for two weeks. But if you need anything. Anything. Go to Hope Hospital. I'll make sure all of your paperwork is there before we go on vacation. You're not due but, with this dizziness you're not concerned about, don't hesitate to go. Okay, Andrea? You are too close to term; let's not take anything for granted."

"Okay, Doc, I don't want you to get upset. I promise I'll go."

"We have been through too much to get careless. I'll see you after the first. Doctor Allen is on call for me. He's an excellent OB. Don't give him any trouble." Doctor Tobias smiled, jotted a few more things on the chart.

She dropped the chart in the slot, "The nurse will be right with you."

"Thanks, Doc. Have a great Christmas. See you after the New Year."

The Doctor closed the door leaving Andrea staring at the ceiling.

Andrea thought, she's right. I should have mentioned the dizziness. Why didn't I? She brought her hands to her tummy, gently rubbed.

She whispered at her tummy, "I'm sorry, Sweet Basil, I'll protect you better when you're out. I promise."

Christmas 1975 gave way to New Year 1976. Andrea limited herself to sedentary activities, reading books, or reorganizing recipes. The dizzy spells were more frequent, and she ultimately told Jason. He was outraged. But his love for her turned the outrage to understanding. Now, he became her shadow. He knew her breathing sounds. If the pattern changed, he would immediately ask, "Are you all right?" Andrea loved his closeness.

She had always been an independent woman. These limitations were challenging, but Jason's unconditional love made the difference.

Andrea's wonderful experience started to turn sour. Her bright green eyes
didn't look as bright. Her dark brown hair lost its luster, and even her fingernails turned brittle. All of this appeared to happen overnight.

Then on January second, a single phone call changed their world.

"Hello, Andrea?"

"Yes."

"This is Doctor Tobias. I know I'm scheduled to see you Thursday, but I just received your lab results. Something is wrong. I didn't want to say anything on your last visit until I received some lab confirmation. I suspect you have uterine cancer." Doctor Tobias heard only a gasp, asking, "Are you all right?"

"Is the baby okay?" "Yes. Normal growth. Everything seems okay with the baby. If you want, we can do a C-section anytime, or we can wait for your due date. I would prefer we do a C-section. Vaginal delivery may be risky; this way, the baby and tumor can come out simultaneously. We can't tell too much right now. If you promise me to stay in bed, you can stay home; otherwise, I'll admit you to Hope."

"I prefer to stay home. Trust me, as soon as Jason hears this. He will make sure I stay in bed."

"I'll see you Thursday without fail. Bye." Doctor Tobias hung up.

Andrea started to cry. Unable to see the phone cradle through her liquid eyes, she couldn't hang up the phone.

Jason quickly came by her side, hung up the phone, and asked, "What happened? Who was it?"

He hugged her; not knowing what was wrong, he asked, "Please, what's wrong?"

Catching her breath, Andrea explained what Doctor Tobias had just said Jason turned pale white.

"It'll be all right. It has to be. We'll fight this together like we always do." For the moment, their consoling hugs alleviated some of the anguish.

Jason immediately called for a hospital bed to be delivered.

He moved all furnishings out of the living room; upon the bed's arrival, he directed the deliverymen toward the empty living room. They placed the bed in front of the fireplace.

Andrea was not allowed to get out of bed without his assistance, and upstairs strictly off-limits for everyone, including the housekeeper.

Jason brought a folding bed from the basement, plopped a sleeping bag on it. Placing the phone within reach, programmed it with the hospital number.

He stayed by Andrea's side day and night. Like a baby kangaroo in its mother's pouch, they were inseparable.

FIVE
Jason

Jason drove home by instinct. The colorful Christmas displays, the animated light shows, were a blur. The traffic, the people had no dimensions. Jason saw images, heard sounds. It didn't matter—blotches and static surrounded him. The grief in his heart detached him from reality.

Arriving home, he opened the garage door, parked the car. As if in slow motion, he opened the car door, stepped out, walked through the doorway, entered the kitchen. His body heavy, drained of energy, Jason sustained his head in his hands. The tears returned, he thought, this is not real. My Sage will open the front door any minute. I'll sit by the door, wait for her to come home.

He hastily walked to the living room. He grabbed the overstuffed charcoal-grey leather chair, dragged it to the foyer. He anxiously sat in it, waiting for the door to open. Listen for exciting sounds, joyful sounds of youth. Yes, he would listen, wait. The door will open, Sage clumsily removing her key as usual.

He sat statuesquely, stared at the mahogany door. Hoping the door would open to end this nightmare.

As the minutes turned to hours, Jason clenched his right hand, hitting his left palm.

"Why have I known so much death? Why? All the people I've loved are gone. How can this be?" Despondent, Jason collapsed backward, stared at the ceiling.

The sound of a screeching car startled Jason out of his memories. Could it be Sage finally coming home? The sound of the revved-up car disappeared like echoes into a canyon. Jason stared at the door. Hoping. Praying. Maybe it would open?

No, that conception had been a sham. Jason knew it. Accepting the truth forced him to make a decision, a decision he wanted to put off as long as possible.

Nothing happened—nothing but silence.

Jason rubbed his eyes, slowly smacked his lips together. He looked at his watch, almost three, he swirled his tongue around trying to induce saliva. His mouth had become so dry, licking a stamp would be impossible. He stood, dragged to the bar, poured some brandy. He chugged the liquid, swished it around as he swallowed, relieving his thirst. He poured another snifter of brandy, sipped it this time. Finished the drink, he slowly put the glass down, sluggishly walked back to the overstuffed chair, and sat, his surreal thoughts still with him.

Five years after the discovery of cancer, Andrea died. Tears filled Jason's eyes as he remembered trying to comfort Sage. Her innocent questions deserved answers, and Jason found the fortitude to answer his little girl. He had to. He must preserve and implant Andrea's memory, and his eternal love had to live on for her.

"Daddy, why did mommy leave us?"

"Sage, you're too young to understand death. At your age, you should be enjoying life, not mourning it. Your mother had uterine cancer. After you were born, the Doctor's discovered it. They operated immediately, and all seemed fine until it came back. We didn't realize it until it was too late. Sooner or later, everyone dies and—"

Quickly interrupting, Sage said, "No, Daddy, you will live forever. I will die before you. I won't go through this hurt again. How could Mommy leave us? She was always there, and then she was gone—she betrayed us. She left without saying good-bye."

Jason remembered hugging Sage. Her tears on his shoulder were poison to his heart.

"Sweet Basil, please don't say those words."

Sage shouted, "Don't call me that." After the words came out, Sage realized the pain she had caused.

"I'm sorry, Daddy. Tell me about my nickname—about Mommy."

Jason smiled. Hugged her again, saying, "Your mother studied for three years throughout Europe, becoming a great chef. When she returned to the states, she came back to Chicago. She loved this city. Its movement, its diversity, for her, this was the only place to live.

We met at a restaurant convention. We knew immediately we would start a life together; no one could come between our love. We married on August 10, 1970. Six months later, we decided to open a restaurant. Mom came up with the name. She called it the Runaway. A whimsical name for her type of creative cooking. She loved to run away with different herbs in the simplest of dishes. She would combine spices until the taste created a party in her mouth. Andrea always said, 'The challenge in cooking is to make your taste buds dance. Herbs and quality products will do it every time.' She could make the good old American burger taste like a gourmet meal just by adding her special herbs mixture."

Jason continued as Sage listened attentively. "The restaurant became a huge success, surpassing our dreams. We had something missing. We realized it was time to start a family. Your Mommy got pregnant, and she wanted to dedicate her time and energy to you, so we decided to sell the Runaway.

Mommy talked to you even before you were born, nicknaming you, Sweet Basil. She instinctively knew you were going to be a girl. Mom would talk to her tummy, saying, "My Sweet Basil, added spice to our life.

A simple spice that marvels the palate and stimulates the appetite. In the case of my Sweet Basil, the appetite for life."

"Daddy, please stop. I can't listen anymore. I'll miss Mommy forever."

"Sweet Basil, that's okay. Your mother enjoyed life to the fullest. Don't tarnish her memory with words like betray. Remember her for her passion evoked in her lifetime. She has only left us physically. Her memory will remain with us always, and because of you, she still lives."

"Daddy, you dried up my tears. Good-bye Mommy. I love you."

On those memories, Jason knew what he needed to tell Sage. Exhausted, drained of all energy, he thought, I must say good-bye. The thought of saying farewell to Sage brought him sadness and eventual tranquility. Saying it out loud gave him the courage.

"I must say good-bye."

SIX
Sage

Trying to wake up, Sage gently rubbed her eyes. Listless, she rolled onto her stomach. I shouldn't be lying here. Am I supposed to be doing something? What is it? I can't remember.

She propped her head on her hands and looked around. Things were not familiar. Quickly turned over, she sat on the bed. Everything seemed real, yet some vision. Am I dreaming? She looked at her body and realized she was naked, astonished at how pale and mottled her body appeared. Shouldn't I be cold? Surprisingly she did not feel cold. She poked her thigh, leaving an indentation.

"I didn't feel that. Why? There's a mark. I've never left grooves on my body by touching it; this can't be happening." Her voice somehow sounded eerie.

She continued to touch her body, kneaded the same spot, leaving finger ridge marks, like playing with clay. She could see the patterns yet felt no sensations.

Sage asked the empty room, "Where are my clothes? Maybe I was getting dressed and fell asleep, or maybe I blacked out? I've never fainted before. Perhaps I drank too much? No, I wouldn't do that."

Remaining very still, she tried to understand. Where am I? Where are my things, where is Rudy? This is not my bedroom.

Sage ran toward the door, attempted to open it, nothing happened. She turned the doorknob several times in both directions—nothing happened. Sage started to pound the door, screaming, "Rudy, open the door; I can't open the door."

Putting her ear against the door, she hoped to hear Rudy's voice. Nothing but scary silence.

Terrified, Sage tried to give herself courage. She thought, if I had a phone, I'd call Dad. He would know what's going on. He would be here without question. Dad would never leave me in a place like this.

Sage walked back on shaky legs like a frightened puppy to the room's only object, an unfamiliar bed. Taking the cold bed sheet, she instinctively covered herself. Hugging her security cover, she seemed to slither onto the strange bed. Sitting in the quietness, it somehow calmed her. It helped her regain bodily strength and mental courage.

Asking the emptiness, "Is this the end of the world and Rudy forgot about me? No, that can't be it. Something happened to him; otherwise, he would be here. I know he would be here.

She sat and stared at the unopenable door.

Slowly the door began to vanish. Sage could not believe what happened. She quickly jumped up, the sheet fell. Her bare ashen body trembled. She could not move. The shock of the disappearing door frightened her, yet quizzical stares invited her. Staring at the spot where the door used to be, she carefully tiptoed to the empty wall. Sage looked for an indication a door had been there—nothing. The door had vanished.

A state of anxiety brought Sage back to the bed. She fanned herself with her hands, hoping it would alleviate her.

"I think I'm hyperventilating," She grabbed the sheet—it faded.

"No! Get control. There has to be a rational explanation?"

She trembled with fear, hoped someone would wake her from this horrible place.

"Where is everybody? Won't someone please help me? How did I get here? Where am I?"

She stared at her hands. They, too, were fading.

"Nooo! For sure, this is not happening. This can't be. Someone is playing a trick. It has to be a trick."

She squeezed her eyes shut. She could see images. Images of someone familiar. Who is that? Who?"

Wait a minute. I remember." She shouted.

Sage jumped for joy at remembering.

"Mother. Mother is supposed to meet me. That's it! Yeah, Mother, Grandmother, and Auntie Rita. Yes, Grandmother's peppermint candy. It will be wonderful."

She laid down again.

Remembering her mother's comforting hug and the soothing voice saying, 'When the good-byes are said, we'll meet again.' That brought her relief; euphoria surrounded her. She smiled.

"Yes, mother said that," Sage confirmed.

She looked around the unfamiliar room, the terror she had imagined gone. The room somehow invited her now. The fear is gone. Everything is clear. Mother. She remembered.

"I'm so tired."

She rolled onto her left side closed her eyes. Nothing else mattered. The fading objects, even her fading body, didn't matter.

Remembering the peace mother had talked about came again, like being in the gondola of a gas-filled balloon soaring high above the cloudless sky. The whispering winds softly and gently guiding her to tranquility. She slept.

SEVEN
Jason

S lowly waking, Jason found himself in the overstuffed chair. Staring at the mahogany door, he rubbed his temples. He thought, did I sleep? I'm exhausted.

He had a horrendous headache.

The desperate hope to see the door open had gone, like the winds of a hurricane dying at sea. The stillness of the house brought back the sadness inside of him. He rose from the chair in a stupefied state, slowly ambled upstairs to freshen up.

Approaching Sage's room, he stopped, opened the door, and tiptoed inside. He hoped to see his daughter in her bed sleeping, safe. He stood by the bed and stared. He softly caressed an imaginary form on the empty bed. He cautiously sat on the edge of the bed like walking on a frozen pond in late autumn. Feeling Sage's presence, he didn't want to disturb her.

Thoughts of Rudy and Ms. Julia made him furious. Telling the empty bed, "I have never hated anyone in my life. Rudy brought this horrible emotion to my conscience. Your meaningless death has destroyed me. How can I ever love again?"

His fist punched the bed with fury. Putting his soaked tear face into Sage's pillow, he cried until his eyes could not cry anymore.

He sat on the bed, drained of all emotion. He had to find the willpower to go back to the hospital. He inched his way off the bed, gazed at the vacant sleeping space. He slowly walked out of Sage's room, closing the door

36

behind him. He would never open the room again.

Jason stepped through the corridors of the hospital. His walk, endless as the ocean on a hot August day. Reaching room one fifty, Jason stood in front of the door, his heart racing, knowing what he had to do. He took a deep breath and pushed the door open.

A young nurse stood near Sage's bed, adjusted the IV's, looked at the monitors, updated the chart. She smiled at Jason as he approached.

"Hi, Jason."

The nurse had much experience working in the ICU. She felt Jason's agony. She finished annotating the chart, put it in the bed slot, and quietly left the room.

Jason did not hear a word. His attention solely riveted on his daughter. He stared at Sage, hoped to see movement or maybe her beautiful smile. He gently stroked her forehead. She looked so innocent. He started to talk to her.

"My dear Sweet Basil, why didn't you listen to me? You went too fast. If I had known this was going to happen, I'd never approved of you moving out. I tried to tell you Rudy was no good. The egotistical coward. How could you love someone like that? I know it wasn't love. You're too young to know love. Love happens through time. The time you don't have anymore. The time that cowardly bastard stopped for you. And me. I'll never forgive him! He let you die; he took you away from me. He robbed me of grandchildren. Of your mother's heredity. Of your trips and adventures. Rudy should be in this room dying, not you. Not you."

Jason slowly bent toward his comatose daughter. He gingerly kissed her forehead for the last time, traced her delicate face for the last time.

In a compassionate harmonic voice, he said the words he had to say.

"Good-bye, Sage, my Sweet Basil, good-bye."

Part Two
Unconditional Love
"I must understand."

EIGHT
Andrea

Looking at her daughter, Andrea smiled. Sage opened her tired eyes and saw her mother.

"Mom? Is that you, or is this a dream? I see you. You're beautiful."

Sage touched her face.

Andrea knew she felt nothing.

Sage shouted, "It's a nightmare. I'm having a nightmare."

She continued touching herself. Feeling no stimulation, she started to panic.

"What's happening? Daddy, where are you? Help me. Somebody, help me." She screamed.

Andrea knew once they performed the guiding ritual, the physical sense of touch would not matter. Calmness would return.

When life as we know it leaves the physical body, it is overtly traumatic. But when the soul lingers in a decaying body; the soul becomes disoriented. The life and death world the soul has endured is the sufferings of nightmares. The trinity has to come together forcefully to bring the soul where it belongs, in the catacombs of the afterlife. The forceful joining adjusts the transition bringing the soul to blissfulness.

"Yes, Sage. It is mother. Don't say another word; try to stay calm.

Before you are of this world, I must bring the trinity."

A doorway opened, in walked Grandma Jenny and Auntie Rita. The three
images forcefully joined hands, creating life-giving sparks. They surrounded Sage with a loving, energetic spirit. The three had to breathe on Sage's fading body gently.

In unison, they chanted, "Enter the world of the spirit with life everlasting."

Without this simple ritual, the soul would be lost. Grandma and Auntie smiled radiantly, looking upon Sage slowly regaining her physical appearance. Not uttering a word, they softly broke the circle and left the room.

Sage, tired, elated, and anxious, sat saying, "Mother, please explain before I wake up."

For the moment, Andrea's soothing radiance dissipated Sage's anxiety. Her mottled, earthly body, now entirely ashen pale like cold lava.

"Sage. Please listen; since the beginning of death, the new soul has heard this explanation. Yes, your physical body has died. We are spirit energy. The soul only reenters the physical form when selected to guide a new spirit from the physical world.

"The selected soul guiding the new soul is someone you loved, respected, or someone you bestowed kindness to during your life in the physical world.

The chosen spirit guide must form a trinity. The trinity is the energy needed for the soul to leave the dying physical body. Three folds of good positive energy are always required to help a spirit energy release from the physical body. The good-byes from the physical world allow the soul to enter calmly into the catacombs of the afterlife. Without the good-byes, it's a jolt. Scary. Terrifying to some. The trinity must surround the soul longer when no good-byes are said. This simplistic touch allows the soul to find peace and contentment.

The warm breath of the trinity is necessary when a soul lingers in the in-between world. Since the soul has endured on an unnatural plane, the warm spirit breath revitalizes the soul's energy. The trinity breath is astounding.

The chosen guide leads the new soul to the cross over, ready to leave the catacombs of the afterlife. Both souls enter the everlasting world. The discarded physical body, along with all its frailties, is gone. I am an illusion, a façade for your benefit."

Andrea displayed the image of her physical body, the illusion real, indeed a spirit world real.

Andrea continued, "The newly released soul immediately needs to see someone familiar—just as birth trauma needs mothering, so too death trauma. I'm going to show you the appearance of the soul; this is the ultimate state of being."

In an instant, Andrea's body disappeared, releasing her soul, a formless radiant light. The light filled Sage with wonderment and solace. She extended her arms, trying to touch the glowing light. Her hands, through the light, felt the radiant center. A sensation of tranquillity and love exuded within her. Sage closed her eyes, letting the light take over.

"This must be heaven!" Sage shouted.

The light gently flowed through Sage's entire mesmerized body. Andrea floated out, slowly drifted in front of her daughter, reappearing in her familiar physical form.

"Mother. It was wonderful. The peace and love you gave me, incredible. Beyond my understanding until now. Is this the way it will be for the rest of eternity? If so—"

Andrea interrupted, "There is more Sweet Basil. The spirit world is a utopia without a doubt. However, the physical world is just as utopian if one lived to the fullest. You didn't get that chance. The reason you are bewildered, even anxious, is because you died prematurely. You did not live to the point of your existence." She paused to reflect.

"When the physical body begins to die naturally, life turns to existence. Existence is when the physical body is frail, but the soul is robust. When the soul takes over, it is time to let go of the physical body. At the same time, the spirit world is also preparing for the emerging soul. The preparation starts with the selection of one spirit; the Almighty Spirit designates the chosen one. There is always one spirit but not always a trinity. If the guide cannot form a trinity, the soul remains in a lackadaisical space called the oblivion crypt. The crypt is the most wretched place in the entire cosmos. Just three acts of kindness in a lifetime would keep the soul out of this horrendous space. Eventually, the soul's energy dwindles to nothingness.

That is the ultimate state of destruction. True death—the death of the soul. The chosen spirit cleanses the entire space of bad energies. All gone, including memories. The crypt is sealed and vanished."

Sage recalled the embodiment of the light. A smile encircled her radiant pale face.

"Am I in heaven?"

"No, Sweet Basil, you are at the passage. First, giving up the physical body, then crossing from the catacombs. The soul joining the eternal lights is, at last, the final state of pure ultimate goodness and tranquillity. The souls remain there until called upon to guide."

In a sarcastic tone, Sage suddenly asked, "All right, mother, now what?"

The tranquil ambiance of the catacomb became uneasy.

NINE
Clayton

Andrea looked at her daughter's confused demeanor, and it almost made her stop this crazy notion. We should cross over and stop the pain. Instead, she gently stroked Sage's hand, patiently waited for calmness to return.

Confused, Sage looked around the bare, colorless room. She didn't dare move a muscle, rolling her eyes around, managed to get a look at the surroundings. She didn't see anything. Her thoughts shouted, scrambled, didn't make sense. What happened? Where am I? Mother? This is a DREAM.

"Mother? Daddy?"

"Yes, Sage, Mother is here. You'll be fine in a moment. You had to go back to sleep. Antagonism in any form is not acceptable. Negative thoughts and emotions are forbidden. Angry words are not tolerated, especially comments of enmity; they hurt the soul beyond repair."

Sage listened to her mother's words realized this was not a dream. Remembering, she had died, spirit energy now, this angelic room the place to meet.

Andrea solemnly continued, "Every individual has bad emotions, some more than others. The catacombs are a place of transition and purification. The first transition is the physical body and soul detach— releasing bad emotions. As steam billows from a boiling teapot, so do emotions, and the catacomb filters out all bad emotions. The second transition allows the soul to become purified. Only goodness remains. The soul is ready to cross over," Andrea looked lovingly at Sage.

She continued, "Regrettably, being in the physical form, it isn't easy to control our emotions. You are in a delicate state like a magnet grabbing metal particles; newly released souls can easily grab threatening emotions. The transition to goodness is not truly complete until the cross over. The longer we remain in the physical form, the greater the chances of exposing coercive ideas. Telltale signs of bad emotions linger like smoke, jeopardizing paradise. That's why we must find the entrance; by the time we find the doorway, bad emotions have vanished."

Andrea took a deep breath, slowly exhaled, relieved her phantom body of the last negative energy explaining, "Such horrible emotions tire the soul. If I need additional good energy to help fight these adverse emotions, Grandma Jenny or Auntie Rita will help."

Still groggy and dumbfound, Sage mindlessly shook her head up and down. She took a deep breath, hoping the grogginess would soon subside.

Sage said, "I understand, Mother. So when do we cross over?"

In her docile, loving manner, Andrea said, "Let me explain why I'm willing to go to the edge of no return. I know I am gambling with your existence."

Befuddled, Sage said, "Mother, I don't understand. You are frightening me."

Aroused with excitement, Andrea explained, "Your premature death allows me to give you the experience of the physical world again."

"You mean I can go back to Daddy. I can be with Rudy." The thought of being with Rudy again clearly made Sage giddy with excitement.

"Not exactly go back to Daddy or Rudy. Sweet Basil, even in death, my love for you is unconditional. Because of this love, I want you to go back. So you, too, have a chance of knowing unconditional love and living life to the fullest. Giving of yourself to others, maybe change the destiny of those you encounter. I must remind you, the choices you make continually change destiny."

Fretful, Sage could not hold back.

"Mother, I don't want that burden. Most of the time, life sucks. Look at you. You didn't grow old with Daddy or see me graduate." On the edge of insolence, Sage stopped talking.

Andrea responded with compassion, "Sweet Basil, I lived life to the fullest. I did not die prematurely—you did. I'm going to tell you about your life if you and Maggie had fulfilled your dreams. Your innocent youthful dreams. You would still be in the physical world, living life to the fullest. You would have lived to be eighty-five years old. Your point of existence."

Clayton wept as he looked at the little angel; he had to look away quickly. He didn't want to startle the baby. His stare looked up.

"At that moment, Andrea should have stopped. She should have forgotten about this crazy idea. She should have realized where she was at, the catacombs. The catacombs are a sanctuary of glory and exaltation or agony and sorrow. Andrea neglected all the rules, and her unconditional love clouded her judgment. They should have crossed over immediately." He looked up again, trying to regain composure.

Clayton hugged the little angel. He continued trying to understand the event that took his beloved family as he continued conversing with the little angel.

"Nothing in life is predestined. Life's turns change quicker than a tornado's path. That's the beauty of life. Staying in bed a second longer may change the course of your life. Why was Andrea so convinced she could change destiny? I don't know, little angel. I don't understand Andrea's motives. I must understand."

TEN
Andrea

The catacomb, now blissful, Andrea proceeded to tell Sage about the life she may have lived.

"Rudy left the party with his friends. They decided to go bar hopping. A little past midnight, you went home.

A month later, World Airlines offered you a job. Rudy couldn't handle that. He knew he would lose control of you. Then you were scheduled for an overseas flight. Rudy didn't want you to take the assignment, and he wanted you to quit. You managed to tell him no. You took the flight and broke-up with Rudy a few weeks later.

After a year of being a flight attendant, you and a co-worker, Fran, collaborated in opening a travel agency. You and she worked twelve-hour days. It paid off. The two of you enjoyed a profitable business venture.

Three years later, you met Steve Logan, a handsome twenty-eight-year-old. He had curly, light-brown hair highlighted with golden blond streaks—irresistible light-blue almond-shaped eyes.

Steve walked in, looking for a bargain round-trip airfare. He needed a flight from Chicago to New York for a job interview, just starting in his law career.

Steve was immediately at ease with you. "I can't afford much now, but if I get hired at this law firm, all my sacrifices were worth it. I need a bit of luck now."

You listened about his previous interviews and how hard it has been to get into a respectable law firm.

"I have a pass to New York. I know I can't use it, neither can my partner. The pass expires at the end of the month. They're not first-class, but the price is right."

"I'll take it," Steve said without hesitation.

"I hope I'm your lady luck. Maybe we can meet after you come back. I have friends at the Chicago Bar Association. Please don't say yes until you meet my contact. I know Judge Russell. I do all her travel plans. I'm sure she would help you find something here in Chicago."

Steve came back. He had refused the job. The two of you got married on September 8, 1996.

A year later, you had a baby girl, Samantha. Then a year after that, a baby boy, Zachary. The children were the light of your life. They go through the typical childhood diseases. A few shaky moments with Zack, when he was two years old, he stepped on a sharp rock. It cut the bottom of his right foot. You wrapped his foot in a towel, grabbed Samantha, and drove to the hospital. He received three stitches. After that, he never went outside without shoes.

Samantha grew to be a gorgeous and joyful person. She had beautiful dark-auburn, wavy, shoulder-length hair. Her most attractive features were her eyes, just like yours, Sweet Basil, big beautiful green eyes.

She graduated from high school and went to the University of Urbana. She majored in music therapy. In her senior year, she met her future husband, Derek Shore. A rugged-looking young man of twenty-four years. He bore red hair fashioned in a buzz cut, also, his senior year. He majored in aquatic therapy.

Samantha thought that combination, water therapy, and Shore was hilarious. When she introduced him to you and Steve, she said, "Mom, Dad, I'd like you to meet Swima Shore."

Taken aback by the introduction, Derek exhibited a rosy red complexion highlighting his big brown eyes. Samantha was in hysterics.

"Just kidding, his name is Derek Shore, majoring in aquatic therapy."

Immediately you and Steve started to laugh too. It turned out to be a great first meeting.

Derek and Samantha married. They had three children, Leroy, Adam, and Daniel. You and Steve were there to listen, comfort, and advise them in the ups and downs of raising children and about life in general.

Zack, on the other hand, not as level headed. He had light-auburn hair and big amber eyes, and a sturdy built but boyish looks. His fate was not a happy one, but he lived life to the fullest.

Two years after high school, he wanted to explore the world. He joined the Navy. You and Steve were against it, however, supportive of his decision. When he graduated from boot camp, you two were there. Proud as ever. Since he did not have any particular occupation in mind, the recruiter talked him into turbine engine repair, assigning him to a Navy School in Virginia.

Eleven months later, he graduated. Again you and Steve were there supporting him. Samantha came along, too, as Zack was going to be at sea duty for six months. Zack was so excited; he couldn't wait for his assignment, which came on graduation day. The orders read, report to the USS Constellation. He was thrilled when he read the orders. "Word has it that it's the best carrier in the fleet," Zack said with boyish glee. He couldn't wait to start his assignment.

The USS Constellation was one of the best carriers. Along with the best comes demanding and excruciating hard work at all times.

Assigned to a team, they were responsible for maintaining the carrier's engines and the aircraft onboard.

Zack's inexperience with life and zest for adventure, at times, made him do things on impulse.

He and Bruno were on duty. They had four more hours of their twenty-four-hour shifts. They started goofing around to stay awake. Bruno dared Zack to blow smoke at the birds nesting in the aircraft engines while hanging from a rope.

With the vigor and daring of youth, Zack climbed the rope. Not to be outdared, Bruno twirled the rope from below. Both laughed like kids at a playground. Suddenly a bird swooped out of the engine compartment pecking Zack's eyes and face. Zack lost his grip. He fell and died instantly. Bruno, beyond himself, started to scream unmercifully. A petty officer rushed over to help and console him.

Bruno pleaded with the commanding officer to let him tell the family. The commanding officer agreed if Bruno signed an early discharge.

Bruno appeared at your door, recounting the terrible incident of Zack's death.

The family made arrangements for the funeral, more than two hundred people came to his wake. It overwhelmed everyone.

That evening Bruno committed suicide. He left you and Steve a note. He wrote, 'If I cannot share my life with Zack, maybe I can share in our death. Thanks for your understanding. Good-bye, Bruno.'

Ostracized by his family long ago, you and Steve took care of his funeral arrangements and laid him to rest next to Zack.

Lovingly looking at her daughter, Andrea paused for a moment, then said, "However, the decision you made to go with Rudy changed your destiny. Samantha and Zack will exist, but with different parents. Their destinies also changed as yet their fates unknown."

Sage, unable to control herself anymore, screamed, "No stop. You can't be right. That's not the way it happened. Rudy loved me. I gave him all of myself unconditionally. I lost my virginity to him."

"Are you implying I'm lying? Why would I lie to you?" Andrea became livid.

A portal in the catacomb opened. Andrea's mother, Jenny, came through. No time for words, she promptly put Sage to sleep, swiftly ushered Andrea through the portal.

Opposing forces sparkled throughout the catacomb, strong forces causing explosive death to the body. Negative forces ready to pounce on the soul like a hungry cat on a bird.

Jenny's goodness had averted their destruction.

This time.

ELEVEN
The Catacomb

The abrupt departure made the warm essences of the catacomb frigid like the setting sun on a late winter evening. Sage's chilly soul had a faint glow. Her physical body slowly faded.

Andrea entered just in time to help Sage rejuvenate her soul. Bringing back the ghostly physical body required deeper concentration. Andrea willed her daughter's soul back to existence. She gently touched the apparition and delicately breathed life on the fragile body.

The catacomb had goodness. The catacomb had life again.

Sage slowly began to stand—out of her daze, her frail body trying to recuperate from the deep, sudden sleep.

"Mother?" Sage asked in a quiet and humbling manner. "Did I mess up again?"

"No, it wasn't your fault. I made a mistake; I started to feel rage. Negative emotions are powerful. We were on the edge of prohibited emotions."

"You mean I can't state my opinion without being put to sleep each time?" Sage asked cautiously.

"Sweet Basil, you can say anything you want. However, positive emotions have to outweigh negative emotions. A contrary opinion doesn't have to be adverse."

In a quiescent manner, Andrea continued.

"Please explain your idea of unconditional love. First, I must warn you.

We only have one more backup. Auntie Rita. Our emotions are at a peak. We must
control them. There can only be one more outburst. Do you understand?"

In a docile manner and with a wide-eyed innocent look, Sage stared at her mother and said, "I think I understand. If Auntie Rita enters, it's nap time again."

Andrea smiled, looked at Sage with patience and understanding. The kind of patience tolerated by unconditional love. She overlooked her daughter's simplistic explanation. Andrea did not want to think about Auntie Rita appearing; that occurrence terrified her. Instead, she desired to hear her Sweet Basil explain unconditional love. She intended to savor being in the catacomb with her innocent daughter.

"Stop," Clayton shouted. "Why didn't she stop? She should have explained the consequences. If Rita appeared, it would be true death for Sage's soul; destructive emotions—gone too far. You can't have negative ideas in the catacombs.

The soul's transition to goodness is cleansing a lifetime. Allowing the soul to dwell on negative emotions uses up precious loving energy. Andrea began playing Russian roulette. She should have known her unconditional love started to turn deadly. Why didn't she stop?"

Clayton's wails startled the baby. So much so that he began to whimper and squirm. Clayton knew his time would shorten quickly if the baby angel cried. The baby's peaceful demeanor had extended Clayton's time safely in the catacomb. No baby angel suffers in the afterlife. Ever. The cries jeopardized his safe stay.

Clayton desperately hugged the little angel, hoping to bring back peace and joy. As much as he tried, the baby squirmed. He tried to remember a lullaby.

The baby grimaced, his bottom lip shaking, on the verge of a scream.

Clayton began to sing Amazing Grace, affectionately massaged the baby's feet, "and grace will lead us home."

The baby's frown became a smile. At last, the baby's eyes sparkled again.

The hymn soothed the baby and Clayton. The little angel slowly nodded to sleep. Clayton sighed with relief, continuing to massage the baby's feet.

Apologizing to the little angel for the outburst, Clayton warily remembered
they were in the catacombs of the afterlife.

He cautiously persevered with his thoughts as. he had to understand this entire mess.

TWELVE
Sage

S age began her version of unconditional love with the excitement and vigor of youth.

"Maggie and I sat around my room deciding what we were going to do. Friday night, and we had to do something. I suggested we go clubbing and dancing. We always had a fantastic time dancing.

"No, wait," Maggie said with intrigue and delight. "I just remembered. I saw Buster at the Burger Joint. He told me about a happening party in Uptown. Here, I wrote the address on a napkin. It's in my purse." Maggie reached for her enormous purple purse.

"I guess we're not going anywhere. By the time you find the address in that suitcase, it'll be tomorrow."

Giggling, Maggie retorted, "Sure, but bet the party is still going on."

We laughed as Maggie frantically searched her purse.

"Here it is. The address is sixteen fifty, Ohio, on the eighth floor. This address has to be those excellent apartments in Uptown." Maggie said in jubilation.

"Yeah, wait a minute. You want us to crash a party?"

"Why not? We're both twenty and never crashed a party. Come on. It'll be fun. Who knows, we could meet some great guys and end up marrying them." Maggie laughed hysterically.

"Who will be there?"

"That's the fun of crashing a party! You don't know anyone, and no one knows you. We can pretend to be anybody we want. How about exchange students? We can say we're from," Giggling Maggie thought, "From Thailand," She burst out.

"Thailand? Maggie, the pretend has to be believable. We, don't look, Thai."

"Come on. This is the nineties. We'll put on tons of make-up, and nobody will guess the country we're from."

Snapping her fingers, Maggie pointed her index finger knowingly, said, "I've got a better idea we'll be sisters. Our Dad is VIP. Yes, the President— of Bolivia. What language do they speak there?"

We looked at each other, laughed at the crazy idea.

We started making ourselves beautiful, the kind of beauty only youth can understand. Maggie borrowed one of my new sweaters. Her size three-body looked gorgeous in anything she wore.

While we were putting on tons of make-up and doing our nails, I shouted, "Maggie, oh no. I haven't asked Dad for the car. If I take it, he kinda gets mad."

Jumping off the bed, I anxiously stood by the door, flapping my hands and blowing at the wet red nail enamel. I had only polished eight nails. I couldn't continue.

Softly blowing at her black nail polish, Maggie calmly said,

"Sur-r-re. Your Dad, mad at you. That'll be the day."

Ignoring her remark, I clumsily opened the door with my palm.

"Come quick. I think he's still up."

We ran downstairs to the study, where we saw Dad slightly slumped in his recliner. He did not appear to be sleeping. Maggie stayed by the door as I softly approached Dad.

"Daddy?" I whispered.

"What is it?" He asked in a hazy state.

"May I borrow the car?"

Dad wiggled himself upright.

"What time is it?"

"Almost ten."

"Isn't it a bit late to start going out?"

"Daddy, parties are just getting started. If we were there right now, we would be the only ones."

"Perhaps, but you should be responsible enough to know when to quit."

"Dad, please, I'm an adult."

"You are a new adult, making it my job to remind you of that." He quickly added, "for the rest of your life."

Trying to muffle her giggles, Maggie cupped her mouth.

"You too, Maggie. New adult, stop your laughing."

"Da-a-ad," I said, giggling.

Dad smiled, handed me the keys.

"Thanks. Scan you later."

Maggie and I scampered back upstairs to continue the beauty routine and finish our outfits. We would soon be ready for a night of fun and adventure.

THIRTEEN
The Party

Driving north along Michigan Avenue, Maggie and I listened to the blues on the blaring car stereo.

Interrupting her air saxophone accompaniment, Maggie shouted, "Ohio is the next street. I think we turn right."

"Yeah. Ohio is a weird street. It cuts off somewhere, then starts up again. Then you're in Lake Michigan."

"Lake affect." We shouted in unison, laughing uncontrollably.

Maggie said, "They have weird street parking too. We better start looking for a spot. The address should be around here." Maggie rubbed the sweat off the window, squinted her eyes looking for address numbers.

"Look! Parking," Maggie shouted.

"I can't park there. The space is too small."

"I'll direct you. Slow down."

Maggie jubilantly opened the car door. She stepped out and ran behind the car. I rolled down the car window as Maggie got into position. Near the curb, Maggie started her instructions.

"Okay. Turn your wheels left as far as they'll go. Back up slowly until I tell you to stop."

Hesitant but trusting, I followed Maggie's directions. Oblivious to my apprehension, Maggie continued shouting orders and waving hand directions.

"Okay, a little more. Stop. Now turn the wheels to the right.
Re-e-e-al slow."

The reddish taillights gave Maggie a neon look and reinforced her parking know-how.

"Stop. That's it. You're in, perfect. Woo-woo."

Impetuously I watched the electric window slowly roll up, turned off the car, opened the car door, I managed to squeeze out of the vehicle. Locked and slammed the door shut, I ran toward Maggie. We high fived over the triumphant parking.

"What a duo," Maggie exclaimed.

"Yeah."

"Party time," We shouted joyfully.

We walked, looking at addresses.

"This is sixteen thirty-eight, should be a few buildings up," Maggie said.

We fast-paced to the end of the block. The numbers were sixteen forty-eight, crossing the intersection, huge sixteen fifty numbers stared us in the face. We walked into the building, not knowing the name of the tenants.

Entering the elevator, looking at each other, Maggie pushed the button marked eight. We stared at the flashing numbers, anxiously waiting for the row of lights to stop at eight and the doors to slide open.

"How are we going to know which apartment?" I asked.

Rolling her eyes, Maggie smirked, "We will follow the noise."

Wide-eyed, her answer tickled me—such a simple solution. Maggie was right.

A soft ding sound followed by the doors sliding open; we nervously stepped out of the elevator and walked left toward the noise. We heard music coming from the end of the corridor.

"O-o-o, how exciting," I said.

"Yeah. Let's get ready to jam."

We high fived each other in anticipation of entering the party. "Okay, do we knock or just walk in?" I asked as if this were an important meeting.

"We'll do both. Kinda knock and open the door at the same time." Maggie replied with full confidence.

We approached the apartment door, and Maggie softly knocked and opened the door. We could not believe the people crammed in the room.

In unison, we said, "How rad."

Managing to filter through the room, no one saw or heard us walk in. Did anyone care?

"We might know someone here after all. Look at all these people," Maggie said.

"Yeah, let's fuse."

Starting to inch around the room, we looked for familiar faces. The unbelievable crowd did not thin out. We managed to get to another room, finding it just as packed. This party was the biggest we had ever seen.

Maggie turned to me and just stared; her wow look said it all. We were overwhelmed by the crowd and the excitement.

We spotted Buster.

"Buster!"

He waved as he made his way toward us.

Maggie and I knew Buster for about five years. We stayed in touch after high school. He was the class clown. Everyone thought he would be a great comedian. We expected to see him at Second City someday. His straight, dark-brown hair, always slicked over his head, emphasized his beady brown eyes. His large straight nose added to his comedic appearance. He had a muscular body, hidden by oversized clothes and ever-present suspenders disguised his build.

"Maggie. Sage. Da bomb, you're here. Did you BYOB?"

Maggie stared at him, saying, "You never told me to bring booze."

Staring back at her, "Maggie, everyone knows you always pack your booze to this kind of orgy," Buster said whimsically.

Snapping his suspenders and shaking his head sideways, he raised his hand, pointing his thumb straight up.

"Don't brood. I have enough for all of us. We can always go out for more."

Maggie and I looked at each other, rolling our eyes shouting, "What the hell."

"Follow me to the chill box." He exclaimed. With his index finger up, waving it back and forth, Buster started skipping backward, making the way through the dense crowd. We obediently followed him to the kitchen.

Entering the kitchen, Buster opened the refrigerator. He grabbed three cans of generic beer.

"Rotgut." He said, "But gets you going."

Maggie and I each took an olive-colored can, marked with black lettering, BEER. We pulled the tab and took a swallow; immediately, we gagged. Our eyes opened so wide. We thought they were going to bug out of our face.

"Amateurs," Buster said, hysterically.

He took his can and guzzled the fizzy liquid until it was gone.

"That's the only way to drink rotgut." Laughing and burping asked, "Ready for another?" Crushing the can.

"We'll mingle first," I said quickly.

"Yeah." Maggie agreed.

Unfazed, Buster raised his shoulders and snapped his suspenders, saying, "Just don't drink it warm, or you'll get the farts."

"We'll try to remember that." Maggie chortled. "Nice guy but sometimes so bizarre."

We walked away as Buster started to dance while opening another can.

We looked around the crowded room to see if we recognized anybody else. The immense crowd was weird, squished together. It was difficult to distinguish between the guys and the girls.

Maggie said, "I have to go to the little girls' room. I'll ask this girl. Excuse me, where is the bathroom?"

A deep raspy voice said, "Upstairs and to the right, little girl."

"Thanks," Maggie said.

She giggled, cupped her mouth, trying to muffle her laughter.

"He looked like a girl, huh? Well, I need to go—want to come up?"

"Yeah, I thought he was a girl too. Nah, I'll wait here and look around."

As Maggie made her way upstairs, she disappeared into the crowd laughing. I looked around nonchalantly, looking for a familiar face. A glimpse of someone I thought I recognized. Ginger? I couldn't wait for

Maggie's return. Ginger had been the class valedictorian. What was she doing here? Omigod, Maggie would have a cow. I wondered if she had crashed the party? No way! Too nerdy, she wasn't as daring as us. Or was she?

Waiting for Maggie made me antsy. Should I go up or wait a little longer? I couldn't decide when a voice said, "Hi. I'm Rudy."

"Hi, Sage," I turned and saw a gorgeous hunk before me.

Rudy asked matter-of-factly, "Whom do you know here?"

"So far, I know Maggie and Buster."

"I know Buster. Fun guy, especially after a six-pack of his cold rotgut beer."

We both laughed.

"Do you smoke?" Rudy inquired.

"I'll do a few puffs now and then."

"Well, how about doing some with me?"

His eyes were dark and shiny, and he mesmerized me. My thrills suppressed my apprehensions. I couldn't resist.

"Okay, let's go for it."

I followed him outside to the balcony. He took out a smoke. Lit it, taking a big drag. My eyes opened wide as he handed me the smoke. I froze, unable to take the cigarette.

"What's wrong?"

"I thought you meant regular smokes."

Rudy laughed, said, "This is regular smoke."

Still, passing the hand-rolled cigarette toward me, I started to feel uncomfortable. I became fidgety.

"I don't think I want some. Thanks anyway." I managed to say.

"Relax. You don't have to if you don't want to. Have you ever smoked?"

"Not that kind. I dragged on a Virginia Slims once. No, twice. I didn't like it much. It made me cough too much. I tried another brand, but I didn't like it either."

With the calmness and understanding of a new lover, Rudy affirmed, "There is always a first time. Maybe we can do it another day."

With the ease of a master, he puffed again. He made it look so enjoyable—the temptation to say yes overwhelmed me. Instead, "I've heard smoking that stuff, you lose your memory and even makes you go crazy," came out of my mouth.

Rudy coughed and chuckled. It took him a while to compose himself.

"Maybe when I'm an old geezer, my mind will go. Besides, I'm a casual user. If I know the digs, I'll do it. Otherwise, I won't. I do like to have some stashed in case of a bad day. It's great stuff to help you unwind and mellow out." He slowly exhaled as he finished the smoke.

"The munchie trolls are the thing to look out for."

"Munchie trolls?"

Opening his big dark eyes, he grabbed my arm and growled, "You eat everything, insight."

He made me scream with laughter. Suddenly he kissed me on the lips. It surprised me. I didn't know whether to kiss him back. Instead, I just stared at him."

"Am I too brash?"

"No. I just wasn't expecting it." Trying not to be embarrassed.

Rudy continued. He kissed around my neck, nibbled my ear lobe.

Our lips met again. I wanted him to stop; only it felt perfect. Finally, I kissed him back. Following his tempo made me want more. I had never felt this, lured into wanting more, yet afraid of going on.

"Rudy. Please wait." I began to feel intimidated.

He stopped.

"What's the matter?"

"You're going too fast for me. I need more time to figure this out. These feelings are new to me. I want to continue one minute. Then I'm frightened the next."

Sensing my nervousness, Rudy fell back along the wrought iron railing.

"What's wrong?"

He didn't wait for an answer.

"I like you a lot. I don't want to scare you off. I want you to know me. I want us to see each other again."

"You don't know anything about me, how can."

Rudy interrupted, "I know what I want. I saw you waiting around in this crowd. You stood out like a roaring fire in a dark forest. I knew I had to be with you."

He came closer, gently stroked my hair, whispered, "It's okay, let me be the one to end your fears."

His gaze made me want him; such intensity made it scary and exhilarating. Rudy gently kissed me.

"Let's go back inside. We'll eat and drink something. Maybe that will help. I know it'll help me. I've got the munchies." Smiling so assuredly, he made me smile too. We walked back inside; my legs felt like marshmallows. Rudy, close behind, his hands around my waist, helped sustain me.

The apartment still maxed out as we looked around for a place to sit. Rudy pointed to a small empty corner. We shuffled our way toward it.

"I'll go get us something to drink. Maybe some eats too. Vinney might have something stashed."

"Okay. I'll see if I can find Maggie."

As Rudy made his way to the kitchen, he winked, disappearing into the crowd. His flirting looks immediately made me hot.

I looked around for Maggie. I slowly walked back to where we had been standing. I looked around–nothing.

Beginning to get anxious, I didn't know what to do. Wait for Maggie or go looking for her. People were everywhere. Some had weird spaced-out looks. I saw smiles, but sort of painted on, forced eerie smiles. I continued looking, saying under my breath, "Maggie, where are you when I need you?" I decided to go back to the corner and look from there.

Rudy approached. He smiled, handing me a beer and pretzels. I thought I saw a painted smile? The closer he got, the safer I felt. The thought of the painted smile vanished.

"These are all the munchies I found. Do you wanna go out and grab a bite?"

"I came with my girlfriend, Maggie. I won't leave until I find her."

Rudy gently took my hand.

"I'll help you find her. Maybe she'll want to join us?"

He gave me a quick kiss on my left cheek. I looked down, embarrassed.

"Okay. Maggie's wearing a red sweater and black jeans. She has short, reddish-black hair, dark eyes, slender and cute."

Rudy gently held my chin. Looking into my eyes said, "She won't be tough to find then cause you're the only other cute girl here."

He kissed me tenderly on my lips. My heart started to pound again.

Without control, my body felt hot. Thanks, is the only word I could manage to say.

We started looking for Maggie. Rudy suggested looking on the balcony. Making our way toward the balcony, ready to step out, I waited for Rudy. He met someone and stopped to talk. Suddenly Maggie popped in hurriedly. "Maggie," I said.

Interrupting, Maggie started talking and giggling uncontrollably. "Sage. Where have you been? I came back from the bathroom and didn't find you. I
scanned the room and thought I saw you. I swear someone has a sweater just like the one you're wearing. I went over and tapped you on the shoulder, but it wasn't you. This girl, so cool, not as cool as you, but cool, her name is Monica. You're not going to believe this. She lives here. She and Vinney throw a party at least once a month. They invite everyone in the building so no one will complain. Then they have a free-for-all. So are we crashing a party? I think not. That means we haven't crashed a party yet."

Maggie continued without taking a breath, it seemed. Her words were coming out so fast. It's a miracle she didn't choke.

"Then Monica asked if I had signed in? I didn't know what she meant. I told her, yes, trying to be cool. She explained, they are experimenting on a crazy idea. They're some kind of new breed artist."

I tried getting into the conversation, but Maggie just took a deep breath and continued talking non-stop.

"I couldn't leave it at that. You know me, gotta know, gotta do. I looked for Buster. I found him and asked about signing in. He looked at me and said, 'Follow me.' He took me to an upstairs room. The first thing I saw was the large bright pillows on the floor. Then tripods displaying blank canvas in front of each wall. Next to each tripod were clear containers filled with pens of every imaginable color. Then I saw the walls. Signatures. Signatures everywhere. It sounds weird, but it looks so awesome. You're not going to believe this, even signatures on the ceiling. How do you suppose that was done, weird? I, of course, picked up a red pen and signed in. Come on. I'll show you where it's at."

Maggie grabbed my hand, not waiting for me to say a word, led us straight into the room.

"Come over here," Maggie said. Pointing at her signature, she proudly sang, "Ta-da."

"All right, Maggie," I confirmed, adding applause.

"Take a pen and make your mark." Maggie encouraged fervently.

Picking up a pen, I choose a purple medium-point.

Giddy with excitement, Maggie shouted, "Next to my name."

I walked to where Maggie had signed in, scribed with flair, S-a-g-e. We stood there for a moment, just staring at the accomplishment.

Maggie started an imaginary interview.

"Such talent, such genius. The lines. The color. Tell me and our audience Madame Sage, what inspired your creation?"

Maggie put an imaginary microphone to my mouth—we laughed. Our animated antics were interrupted by Rudy's voice.

"Audacious."

Maggie turned, said, "Yes, it is. And this is a private conversation."

"Maggie." I momentarily stared at her, astonished by her unfriendly behavior. "This is Rudy. We were looking for you. We're going to get something to eat. Join us?"

"I think I'll stay. I can get a ride with Buster." Maggie said, irritated, trying to size up Rudy with her peripheral vision.

She moved closer to me. Whispered protectively, "Are you sure you want to go with this guy?"

"He's all right. I kinda like him. Why are you so uptight all of a sudden?"

64

"Something creepy about him. Can't you feel it?" Maggie whispered.

"He makes me feel good. I like him. We'll talk later, I promise."

Leaving the signing room, Maggie huffed away in the opposite direction as Rudy, and I departed for the Burger Joint.

FOURTEEN
Sage

Puzzled about leaving Maggie and about Rudy, Sage stopped recanting and looked at her mother, saying, "That night changed my life forever. Maggie and I lost a little bit of our innocence and rapport." Sage looked sadly at her mother.

"Yes, it did."

Still quizzical, Sage asked, "Why did I allow that to happen? I loved Maggie. We were friends forever. Forever. We had such great high school dreams. We were going to travel and do stuff together. We couldn't wait to graduate so that we could get our grown-up life started."

On the verge of malevolence, Sage's eyes became watery. She took a deep breath.

Andrea compassionately touched her daughter's boney shoulder.

"The choice you made at that moment changed your direction in life, your opinion of people, including people close to you. That happens. The physical world has many stages. The newborn babe, to teenagers' recklessness, to the maturity of the years, each phase brings newness. Each step is an adventure to be celebrated wholeheartedly. Eventually, a person goes back to their roots. It's just living a full life—the full circle of life."

Sage's voice trembled as she uttered, "The choices I made I thought were good. I had very indecisive feelings. How are you supposed to know about these things? I mean, Rudy gave me sensations I had never experienced. I had loved before, Dad and you, Grandma, Maggie. Even Blanco the dog and Finnigan the goldfish. This, Rudy's love, totally different from anything I had ever experienced. It made me tingly all over. I did not want it to stop. Nobody, not anything, had ever given me those feelings. The choice was easy. Rudy."

"Sweet Basil, emotions and feelings are difficult to decipher. I wish I could tell you there is some secret formula. There isn't one. Life in the physical world is trial and error—no set answers. Finding the balance between veracity and errors is part of living a full life. Some people never attain balance. Life is miserable and complicated in the physical world— because of all the choices. The spirit world has only love. No choices. Everything is in balance."

Andrea stopped, looked at her daughter's confused demeanor, asked, "Now what, Sweet Basil?"

"I just realized that night, Maggie and I began our separate paths. It happened so suddenly. I gave up Maggie, everybody, for Rudy. That made me sad, but my love for Rudy will always be. May I continue my version of unconditional love?"

Startled by her daughter's insolent manner, Andrea nonetheless maintained composure, saying, "You have yet to recognize Rudy's selfish ego and the cause of your premature death. Yes, please continue."

The air of effrontery dissipated, as every time Sage spoke of Rudy, her words were tender, with a starry-eyed look. Sage did not fully understand she had been on the edge of destruction. Sage did not fully understand Andrea's love and calm withstood the hostile forces that were about to intrude on their space.

Sage resumed her interpretation with the ease of innocence.

"We left the party for the Burger Joint. As we sat in a booth, a waitress came over and asked if we were ready to order.

Rudy answered without hesitation, "I'll have a double cheeseburger, fries, and a large cola."

Astonished by his quick order, I said, "I'll have anything uncola."

The waitress departed.

For the first time, Rudy and I sat alone with each other. I started getting nervous. At the same time, I wanted him. I told myself, he is a great looking guy, funny, self-assured. Relax already.

"Aren't you hungry?" Rudy asked.

"No, just thirsty. Do you know Monica and Vinney?" I asked, trying to hide my nervousness.

"Yeah. I've known Vinney since grammar school. Monica is the artist. She's mentioned her signing room, as you two called it, as a representation of heaven and hell. After every available space of the room is signed, she will make individual adobe frames to sell at a show. Buy a small portion of heaven or hell. She claims a signature is the only remaining part of a person. She can go on and on about it. Do you wanna hear a secret?"

"Sure, if it isn't too risqué."

"Vinney is not his real name. His real name is Marion. He hates that name. If you ever want to get him mad, I mean ballistic mad, call him Marion. His Mom is the only person on the planet that can call him that name. Was that too risqué?" Rudy asked with a smile.

Nudging his arm, at the same time, saying, "Stop it," as I laughed too. My apprehensions quickly disappeared.

Rudy said, "Sage, I like you a lot, and I want to see you again and again. I'm twenty-six. Next year I'll finish school with a degree in architecture. I live in an apartment above my parents' house for now. Hopefully, I'll move out soon. My mother is overbearing when it comes to me. I know it, but I appease her for peace. My Dad fazes her out. My favorite color is black, but any color you wear is my favorite color. I enjoy traveling and have loads of fun. Now, you know me. I want you to totally no me."

Rudy gently kissed my hand as the waitress brought glasses of water.

Staring at him, I didn't know what to say. He beguiled me, making my insides melt like an ice cream cone in ninety-degree weather. I felt tingly again, then said, "Don't you think you're going too fast?"

Immediately he replied, "Sometimes you have to take life by the balls and go for it," At the same time, he clenched his fist and imitated a grabbing motion.

"Rudy. I was always protected. It's difficult for me to make sudden decisions. I wish I could be more impulsive. I'm not."

The waitress returned. She placed the food in front of Rudy and gave each our drinks.

"Anything else?" She said, smacking her gum.

"No," Rudy said.

"Pay at the cashier when you're ready. Enjoy your meal."

Putting down the check, she winked at Rudy and departed.

"I'm starving." Rudy ravishingly started to eat his burger.

"You must be," I said, sipping my ginger ale.

"I told you. Beware of the munchie trolls." Rudy chuckled as he devoured his meal. "So tell me about yourself."

"Not much to tell. I live with my Dad; my mother passed away when I was little. Daddy is always telling me about her—and I want to be a flight attendant. I start school in a couple of months. My Dad has a cousin in the business. Well, sort of, she's a travel agent. I work with her when help is needed. She's the one who convinced me, not that I needed much convincing. I've had the desire, and I just needed a little push to confirm it. I love to dance."

"Stop. Say no more." Rudy interrupted. "I like to dance too. Let's make it happen. We'll go dancing next Friday or Saturday."

I thought, why not? How else am I going to get to know him? "Okay, let's go dancing."

"Sweet," Rudy replied with enthusiasm. "We'll go to the Silly Goose. Have you ever been there?"

"No, I haven't."

"You'll love it. It's a great place to have some laughs. Are you ready to vacate this place?"

"Sure."

"Can you pay for this?" Rudy asked matter-of-factly.

"Easily."

As I paid, Rudy went to talk to some guys sitting at a table. One guy appeared to have a painted smile; it must be my imagination. This is a public place.

69

After I paid, Rudy met me by the door. We strolled back to the car.

"Hey, I've got half a weed, want to share in some?" "No thanks. I'm driving." I said, as my apprehension rose again.

We stopped walking.

"Sage, I don't want you to feel pressured about anything. I want you to loosen up when you're with me, that's all. I want your trust and confidence. Most of all, I want to become a part of your life."

He smiled irresistibly and tightly hugged me. I felt sensational. He twirled me around as if we were dancing in the moonlight. I laughed. His closeness made me giddy—I wanted him in my life too.

Getting into the car as I drove him home, Rudy channel surfed the radio, said, "You're a great chauffeur." As he took a last drag on the bogus cigarette, "This is my chateau. Want to come up?"

"It's kinda late. I better not."

"Okay. One last kiss to last until I see you again."

Rudy moved closer—his lips embraced mine. They were lustrous, soft, and delectable. I felt titillating sensations I had never felt. The kiss mesmerized me. He slowly eased off.

"That will keep me going until next time." Rudy said provocatively.

"Right, you are," I thought. Is this what it feels like to kiss a movie star? The tingly feeling became explosive. I wanted to shout, don't stop.

Rudy affectionately kissed my hand, as if expressing, to be continued.

"I'll call you later. You'll be in my dreams until then. Good night."

Slowly he closed the car door, winked, turned, and walked away. I watched him walk to the doorway and disappear into the house.

Driving home, I thought only of Rudy. Enthralled by the encounter, I went home in a dream.

I parked the car in the garage, and my thoughts were of Maggie. I had to call her later. Maggie will freak out when she hears of this adventure.

Bedazzled by sleep and unknown feelings, I absentmindedly went to my bedroom. Collapsed on the bed with ruminations about the night, I drifted off to sleep thinking–Rudy.

Clayton nodded his head in disbelief at recalling that incident. He couldn't help it.

He asked the emptiness, "Why didn't Andrea tell Sage none of this mattered? As soon as they crossed over, the memories would be gone. This is as far as all memories go. The catacombs filter everything out of the new soul. Nothing of the past life endures at that moment. It would be maddening to have memories linger for the rest of eternity. Now, once you've been at this as long as I have, and Andrea, too, recollections come in snippets. That's why Andrea, myself, and the family are in this predicament—snippets of life.

The physical body brings the memories. A glimmer of memories appears each time a soul returns to the body. In the catacombs, that is a lifetime.

Andrea, why did you forget that?"

Clayton told himself to stay calm. Looking at the innocent angel helped his temperament. Singing the third verse to Amazing Grace helped him continue his passionate search for understanding and inner peace.

FIFTEEN
Sage and Maggie

I laid in bed blankly staring at the ceiling, trying to decide if Rudy had been real or a dream. He had to be real. I could still smell his presence.

I sat up thinking of Maggie. I quickly rubbed my eyes, grabbed the phone, and instinctively dialed her number. While waiting for an answer, I noticed I still had on the same outfit. What happened to my pajamas? Wow! It must have been some night. I giggled at the thought as a groggy voice sounded.

"Hey, Maggie. Are you awake?"

"I guess I am. Sage?"

"Yeah. I have to tell you about last night, about Rudy."

"Wait a minute. What time is it?" Maggie asked in a lethargic tone.

"I don't know. Let me see. It's four a.m."

"Four, huh? Hold a sec."

Listening to the silence, remembering Rudy and the fantastic feelings, I impatiently waited for Maggie. For the young, an eternity had passed.

"Okay. I had to splash water on my face." Maggie said, her voice now energetic and alert.

"There is so much I want to tell you, I don't know where to start," Sage said, as her mind went from thought to thought.

"Where did you go after the party?"

"We went to the Burger Joint. Rudy told me all about himself. He's a student and told me about his parents, his wants, his dislikes—everything, and he wants to be a part of my life. He is so sure of himself. Oh, the way

72

he kisses! It's magical. Every time he came close, I wanted him closer. I wanted to freeze the moment."

"Hey, wh-o-o-o-a. Speed bump! I can't believe what you're saying. You're always so level-headed and cautious. What's going on? Did you do it?"

"No, we didn't do it. I don't know what's going on with me. That's why I had to talk to someone. I don't understand this—these feelings—I'm in a fantasy when Rudy's around. He makes me gush and soar at the same time. I think about him and wonder what's going on? He's all I've thought about, and I went to sleep thinking about him."

"You mean you've slept?"

"I think I did. I haven't put on my pajamas. I'm still in my street clothes, and you know how I love my pj's."

This outrageous conversation made us laugh. Talking to Maggie was always fun.

"Rudy and I are going to the Silly Goose either Friday or Saturday night. Join us, okay?"

"The Silly Goose?" Maggie said in a devilish tone. "I guess if you're going on the wild side, that's the place to start."

"What do you mean?"

"I've never been there, but I've heard it's a rowdy joint. Even a warning to females not to wear anything too short."

"Rudy said it's a fun place to go for a good time."

In her know-it-all's voice, Maggie said, "I heard it from Buster. You know, if that kook says, warning, there's truth to it. But it is supposed to be a fun place. Sure let's go."

Maggie stopped talking for a second to catch her breath.

"Let me tell you about my night at Monica and Vianney's. When I came out of the bathroom, I looked everywhere for you. I saw people coming in and out of the balcony; I thought you might be out there. Stepping out, I smelled a funny odor. I didn't recognize it, but it was somewhat earthy-sweet, like the smell of a freshly cut lawn after a rain shower. I looked around. The fresh air did feel good. When someone handed me a little pipe, thinking, what the hell is this? I took it and puffed it, which made me choke a little. I didn't want to look like I didn't know what I was doing, so I held it back as much as I could. Some guy next to me reached for the pipe. He couldn't wait for that pipe to be in his hands. The guy was in his world. I gently passed the pipe as calmly as I could. I wanted to get rid of it. I couldn't hold my breath any longer. My cheeks looked like a puff fish, I decided, the hell with it, and coughed out the smoke.

I started catching my breath when the damned pipe was being handed to me again. Oh crap! I didn't want anybody to think I'm a dweeb, so I tried it again—the second time. This time I didn't cough as much. I can't remember how many times that thing came around. You talk about feelings. Wow! I couldn't believe the sensations I was experiencing. Everything seemed like it was going in slow motion, yet going fast. It seemed like I was talking ninety words a minute, but nothing made sense. I laughed so much it brought tears to my eyes, but I don't know what was so funny. After a while, my mouth went dry. I mean Arizona dry, I had to have a drink. Someone passed some liquid; that's all I craved. I grabbed it and drank. I had to quench my thirst.

I can't remember how long I was on the balcony. I don't think I puffed right cause I wasn't at the level the others were. They wanted to sit and stare into space.

Then everybody started to look different, weird. That's when I decided to get back inside."

"I know what you mean. When I looked for you, I thought people had painted smiles. I got an eerie feeling too," Sage whispered.

"I didn't get an eerie feeling, but painted smiles? Yeah, that's right, painted smiles." Maggie validated the mental image.

"When you met Rudy, you thought he was eerie." Reminding Maggie of her actions.

"I met Rudy?" Maggie asked.

"Yes, and you were not friendly. Now I know why. When I first saw you coming in from the balcony, your expression had a hint of a painted smile. At the time, I dismissed it thinking it was because I had just seen so many faces with that expression. Please, Maggie, promise you won't do that stuff again."

"That didn't take long. There's your old cautious self again." Maggie said with irritation in her voice.

"I know. Only I don't want you to go brain dead. I don't want you to change. We've been friends for so long, Maggie, that stuff will change you. Promise me."

"Okay, okay. I have to go," Maggie said without promising.

"You're right. Sorry, I woke you. But I had to talk to someone. All these questions siphoned my energies. Thanks for listening, Maggie. Talking to you
helped. Sorry about the hour, I should have waited until later, but my mind was ready to burst. I had to chat with someone."

"Don't give it a second thought. Friends can do this without explanations. You know I hate getting serious, so, see ya when I see ya."

Hanging up the phone, I rolled over, immediately went back to sleep.

Maggie stayed awake, remembering—Rudy had dark, cold shark eyes.

SIXTEEN
Maggie

R udy had not called, making me insane. How could he toy with me? Why didn't he call? Each night I waited for his call. I ached, remembering his touch, his kisses. How could he do this to me? These horrendous notions made the days creep by, making me miserable.

Friday came. By then, I had become edgy. The end of the day could not come soon enough. I thought he'll call tonight. I felt empty, lifeless. How could something this wonderful make me feel so miserable? I became confused. I wanted to hear his voice. At the same time, I desired to choke him, verily confusing.

Home, at last, I stayed in my room waiting for THE phone call. Picking up a magazine, I flipped pages. Not reading, not looking at the pictures, just flipping pages. I threw the magazine down then grabbed my stuffed teddy bear.

I got Bear from Daddy a long time ago. He said to tell Bear anything if Bear didn't listen or have an answer to go to him. He would set Bear and me on the right path.

I rounded out its old ears, carefully straightened the faded yellow ribbon. It stared at me, knowing something was wrong. Bear always knew my feelings, and Bear still consoled me.

I laid down, Bear on my chest, stroking the little paws. The phone rang. I sat up, glared at the ringing apparatus, frozen.

"I know, Bear, calm. Be calm."

My heart pounded faster with each ring. I could feel the blood rush through
my body, like water spewing from a fountain. I became hot. My hands
started to sweat. After the fourth ring, I took a deep breath, picked up the
receiver.

"Hello."

"Hey wanna, crash a party?" Maggie said with gusto.

"Where have you been? I tried calling you a bunch of times."

"Here and there, checking things out., I just got busy. What's going on?"

"I'm waiting for Rudy to call. I haven't heard from him all week. It's
making me miserable. He said he would call. Why hasn't he called?"

Maggie responded with discord in a childish tone said, "Maybe his
mommy won't let him." She then went back to her normal voice, scolded,
"Why are you letting this zero guy make you miserable? Come on, get with
it. It's Friday, let's go dancing, a movie. Anything is better than staying
home and waiting for the phone to ring."

"What if Rudy calls?"

"Sage! Haven't you been listening? He won't get an answer. Big deal,
if he's as wonderful as you say, he'll try again. In the meantime, don't be a
downer. Come on, let's do something! You're going to become an old
grouch if you keep this up. Remember Ms. Anderson, the gym teacher?"

"How could anyone forget, psychojock? You're right. I've been numb
and dumb all week. He made me this way, Friday night, and I'm miserable,
not fair."

My voice started to tremble, and my eyes swelling with tears.

Maggie could feel her misery and became furious.

"This jerk is making you miserable!" She said with clenched teeth.

Calming down, Maggie took a deep breath said, "Come on, your make-
up is going to smear. You're going to get black streaks down your face, and
your eyeballs are going to turn red." Maggie added with cheerfulness,
"You'll be ready for a Kiss concert. Too bad they're not in town."

I started to laugh at Maggie's comments. She made me feel better, and
she had to be right.

In a blink of an eye, Maggie said, "All right, I'll be there in less than an hour. Tonight we will only have a good time. We won't mention what's his name as of now, okay?"

"You're on. See you in an hour."

Talking to Maggie, I realized she was right. Why am I letting someone make me feel miserable? Enough already. Maggie and I will go out and have a great

time. We always do. Maggie is the best friend I'll ever have. She'll never make me miserable. Yeah, Maggie, we won't mention what's his name.

All these thoughts psyched me out for our night out. Except deep in my heart, I still ached for Rudy.

SEVENTEEN
Rudy

Maggie and I sauntered into my bedroom with the vivaciousness and vigor of midday antics.

"What a night. We have to do this again," Maggie exclaimed. "Dancing in different clubs is the best."

Sage murmured, "Hurry, close the door. We don't want to wake up my dad," We laughed as I fell on the bed.

Maggie snorted a laugh, "Remember that guy dancing in the middle of the floor? He looked so intimate and sincere. Too bad he was dancing with a post. You'd think it was his date."

Maggie started mimicking the guy we saw at the Blue Rash Dancing Studio. She grabbed the floor lamp caressed the shade.

"Oh Betty, come to my place tonight. We'll make beautiful light together!" She said in a deep voice.

I became hysterical at watching Maggie's exaggerated farcical movements and her conversation with the Betty lamp. She had the weirdest eye movements, and once she started her eyes, nobody could resist laughing.

Sage once again abjured from her story, asking, "Mother, what happens to Maggie? I can't imagine being without her, not ever seeing her again." Tears flowed from her eyes. "We were friends forever."

"I do not know Maggie's future," Andrea said wearily.

Sage blurted, "Why do you know my future?"

Unruffled, Andrea lovingly looked at her daughter for a moment.

"The future in the physical world is continual. The choices a person makes determines what is to be. I can predict your life cycle because of three conditions. I am a part of your genesis, your premature death, and three, being the most eminent, I pleaded for approbation. Those three conditions are the sole reasons this is possible."

"Perhaps it's better if I don't know anyway."

Reflections of Maggie made Sage teary-eyed again.

"I think I would try to protect her from here. Kind of watch over her." She remarked in a trembling voice.

"That's impossible. The spirit energy cannot interfere with the physical world on a whim. Rarely, a parent can protect their earthly children. That, too, is under strict conditions. Approbation from the Almighty Spirit is always needed. Can you imagine the pandemonium if the spirit world could intercede? Even the pure at heart would find it difficult to refrain from asking something. The harmony existing in the spirit world would cease to exist. It would be chaos, unbalance forces, the inevitable demise of the soul. Sweet Basil, you must understand, negative forces are potent and destructive. The physical world has too many negative emotions and shortcomings. These emotions destroy the physical body. If the spirit energy intervened, the aftermath is the eventual destruction of both entities."

"Why must it be a negative encounter?" Sage asked with cynicism.

"I hope these three words convince you of the destruction of the human soul."

Pausing for a moment to reflect, Andrea said, "In the beginning."

Sage still didn't get it, and she quickly remarked, "Is this some kind of afterlife wisdom? What does that mean?"

"Oh my Sweet Basil, you are so innocent. The physical world has many vices. The temptations created in the physical world are beyond salvation for some individuals. People have forgotten the joy and happiness of life. Everyone is too busy to see the goodness born within. Goodness is in everyone, pure and wholehearted; the difficulty is in acceptance. Since the beginning of death, this is the way it is and the way it will be.

The two worlds dichotomized until the splendor of the revelation."

Dispassionate about the explanation, Sage uttered, "Mother. I understand, except Maggie."

Aghast, Andrea interrupted, "There is NO exception." Struggling to maintain harmony, Andrea closed her eyes, whispered to herself, "Think of the loving light. The peaceful, loving light."

After meditating, she opened her eyes; with aplomb, she said Sage, "Please continue with your saga."

Clayton looked at the baby angel, confounded. He said, "Andrea knew all along about the risks, yet she persisted little one. Oh, but there is more to this crazy disaster, much more. We'll listen."

Aloof about the explanation and interruption, Sage continued.

Being silly at recalling the night's adventures, Maggie and I were doing facials when the phone rang.

"Who could that be at this hour?"

"It's not, me," Maggie quipped. Maybe it's Betty.

We laughed. I picked up the receiver.

"Hello."

"Where have you been? I've been trying to reach you all night." Rudy's tone was acrimonious.

"I waited all week to hear from you. Did you expect me to be sitting here on a Friday night?"

In a whisper, I told Maggie, "It's Rudy."

Maggie angrily rubbed the facial mask off with a wet towel, throwing me a towel. I, too, rubbed off the facial goop.

Maggie signaling to hang up and making gestures of zero, said, "Zero. Zero guy."

I could not hang up. I had to listen. Trying to ignore Maggie, I swatted her hands. Silently I told her to be quiet.

Exaggerated a yawn, Maggie said, "Time for me to be history. Call me later." She left, very annoyed by the interruption.

With Maggie gone, I listened to Rudy more attentively.

"I must explain. I've been trying to convince mother of my feelings for you. It has taken me all week to prepare her."

"Prepare her for what?"

I did not understand the explanation, which made me irate again. And for a split second thought, maybe, Maggie is right—zero guy.

"I told you. Mother is overprotective. She often says her love is unconditional, that no one will give me that kind of love. She goes over the edge when it comes to me. I had to prepare her so you can meet her."

Sounding apologetic now, Rudy continued, "I'm sorry for not calling. Please believe that. Understand, after mother meets you, everything will be spectacular. Come on, Sage, forgive me. I will make it up to you. I promise. Are we still on for the Silly Goose?"

"You tell me," I responded in a frigid voice.

"First, say you will forgive me. I have to hear you say it." Rudy persisted.

I deliberated for a bit and said the words Rudy needed to hear, "I forgive you."

His voice brought giddiness to my temperament. Remembering his touch, I could not resist him. I had to say the words he wanted me to say.

"Audacious. We'll go to the Silly Goose tonight."

"By the way, Maggie is joining us."

"Excellent. The bigger the crowd, the better. Pick me up at ten."

"Okay. See you then. Bye."

Hanging up the phone, I lay in bed with odd thoughts swarming through my mind. Was Rudy sincere? Maybe he just knows what to say? Am I wasting my time? Is Maggie right? Zero guy? Is Daddy going to like him?

The thoughts exhausted me. I inhaled deeply, trying to understand these weird feelings. Stop worrying; everything will be incredible. I smiled, rolled over, thinking of Rudy's delicious touch. His heavenly embrace. Yes, stop worrying.

In a few minutes, the worrisome thoughts faded, like icicles on a warm day. My eyelids, heavy with sleep, slowly closed.

EIGHTEEN
The Talk

Merrily walking into the kitchen, I grabbed a glass and filled it with grapefruit juice. I sat at the breakfast table.

"Hi, Daddy."

"Good morning. What were you two doing last night?"

"What?" I asked, recalling the night's antics.

"You and Maggie had me in hysterics just by your sounds."

We laughed, each for our own reasons.

"You know Maggie, can't help but have fun with her." Grasping the moment to tell Dad about Rudy. "Daddy, I want you to meet someone."

"A special someone? Maybe a boyfriend?"

Astonished by his calmness and intuition, I said, "Perhaps. His name is Rudy. I want you to meet him.

"Tell me when and I'll be ready."

"Thanks, you're the best. We're going out tonight. I'll let you know later."

"Sweet Basil, by the tone of your voice, I think it's time for us to have a little talk. You probably heard this from somebody else already. Now listen to it from someone who loves you dearly, just a few pointers from an old adult to a new adult. First love is exciting, but it can also be confusing. I hope this, Rudy, will treat you with respect and understanding."

"He does, Daddy. He's wonderful. Cute too."

Jason continued, "As I was saying. Respect. I've seen you through various stages of life. Up to this point, this is the one I abhor the most. I can't say read this, and you'll know all about first love. No, with this milestone, I must let you go without a manual, without directions—only your undeveloped instincts. Ironically, the only way to develop them is trial and error. Hoping you won't have too much error along the way. I know you are responsible, and I believe in you. Him, I don't trust. You're my most precious everything. I have to let you go to some stranger so you can learn and grow. I know this happens to everyone. When it happens to the one you love, it's not easy to stand by and watch. It's not easy because I know the probable outcome.

It is at this milestone I wish your mother were here. She would put the finishing touch to this talk. Mom would know precisely what to say. Unfortunately, it is just me.

I know I don't know the real difference between a pad and a tampon; however, I do know this."

Jason reached for his wallet while saying, "Here is something you may need."

He handed me a condom saying, "I hoped you would wait until you married or at least after you started your career. I think that is more important. But of course, I'm the old adult. Since you are the new adult, priorities tend to go in different directions."

Blushing, I said, "Father. Why is that in your wallet?"

"I'm a widower, not a corpse. Besides, it's not my life we are concerned with, and I know what I'm doing. You, on the other hand, just do. Which is good, when do, are constructive ideas. However, when do, is sex, love, or lust, at this point in your life you should not do.

There is nothing wrong with sex, love, or lust, Sage. Except when you cannot distinguish between them. Sex and lust are a young man's desire. Love is a young woman's dream. Eventually, the young adult becomes an older adult things balance out. Getting to that balance is confusing for a new adult. Heck, even some old adults never get to distinguish the difference."

Pausing, Jason stood, saying, "I'm starting to lecture. I don't want to do that. New adults seem to ignore lectures, thinking they know it all. I'm not promising I will like Rudy, but I love you very much. I'll make an effort, try to convince myself you are not a little girl anymore. You're a new adult, a woman, and I have to let you grow. I don't ever want you to grow away from

me. Enjoy life, yes, but not all at once. Most of all, Sweet Basil, no matter what happens, try to tell this old adult about it. More than likely, I've been there."

"Thanks, Dad," I didn't know what to say; as our talk was almost overwhelming, I hugged him.

I went upstairs to get ready for my big night. With all the excitement, I nearly forgot to call Maggie. Picking up the phone, I dialed Maggie's number. It rang five times. Finally, a pick-up. I didn't wait for an answer.

"Hey, Maggie."

"Uhuh."

"Still, joining us at the Silly Goose?"

"Uhuh."

"Are you awake? What are you wearing? Do you want to ride with us?" All these questions and no response. A short moment of silence followed.

"Wait a minute. I think I'm not awake."

"Maggie. Are you okay?"

"Okay, okay, I'm awake. I'm awake."

Rubbing her eyes, scratching her scalp, she continued, yawning and talking at the same time. "I didn't realize I had slept so long. I laid down for just a second," Yawning and stretching, "About six hours ago, I think? When are you leaving?"

"I pick up Rudy at ten."

Irked by that response, Maggie became alert.

"Why are you picking him up?"

"Because he doesn't have any wheels. Why does that bother you anyway?"

"There is something about him. Don't get me wrong. I'm still joining you. Maybe I'll like him better this time around."

"That's my Maggie. So what are you wearing?"

"Probably denim, not sure what top. I gotta see what's in the closet.

You?"

"I'm wearing a black skort with a black and silver top. I bought some black fishnets yesterday, wearing those with my black dancing shoes."

Jokingly Maggie said, "O-o-o-o. How in vogue."

"Do you want me to pick you up?"

"No, that's okay. I'll meet you there. This way, I can slowly get to know him. I'm afraid being in a small space, like the car, I'll be on the defensive."

"What's going on, Maggie? This is not you? You're confusing me."

Melancholy, Maggie said, "You've never been this way with a guy. You're so sensible when it's just us. The minute he came into the picture, you lose it all. This guy is coming between us."

"He isn't coming between us. Rudy is different. He's not like any other guy I've ever met. I like him—a lot. I have never felt this way before. I want to spend the rest of my life with him."

"Did you hear yourself? You want to marry this guy. How can you think of marriage? You don't even know him. We were going to travel, start to have real fun," Maggie retorted, shocked at what she heard.

"I know. This just happened. It's like I'm under a spell when he is around. Maggie, we will always be friends. Forever, remember?"

"I remember. It seems this guy is taking you too fast. We had plans. He was not a part of them."

"I'm lucky I have you on my side. Everything will be awesome, you'll see. We'll all be friends. And when you find someone special, it'll be great. We'll be four best friends. I promise."

"Okay. I won't be so negative. You know I can't stay mad at you. I'll wear a happy top." Maggie laughed.

At the sound of her laughter, I also laughed.

"Okay, I better get going. I'm awake now, and I have a lot to do. I'll meet you there. Bye."

Hanging up the phone, I briefly had bewildering thoughts. Why is Maggie objecting to Rudy? Could she be jealous? I've found the love of my life, and my best friend should be happy for me. It has to be jealousy.

Stop that thinking! Maggie is the coolest and my best friend. This evening Rudy and I will win her over, and she'll like him too. I know it.

Yipes! Time to get going. I don't want to be late, I've missed Rudy too much.

NINETEEN
Forgive me

Driving to Rudy's apartment, thoughts of Maggie were recklessly in my mind. The idea, Rudy coming between us, ridiculous. She needs a little time. Sometimes she's stubborn. I know Maggie; her concept will soon be history. This is new for us. We have shared so much. We have to learn to share ourselves. That's it! As Dad put it, we are new adults. We can't deal with adult sharing, and we'll get it right. Everything will be terrific again.

The closer I got to Rudy's apartment, the more anxious I felt. Turning onto his street, I saw Rudy. Nothing else mattered. I could hardly believe it. He was waiting for me. Exciting.

Rudy stood by the curb. Seeing me approach, he smiled and waved. Slowing the car in front of him, he opened the car door before I came to a complete stop. As he entered the car, he kissed me. The passionate kiss exhilarated me. His touch., his closeness, brought absolute enchantment.

"I've missed you. Hi," Rudy said, slamming the car door.

He outlined my face with his right index finger, ending on my lips. Seductively tracing my lips with his tongue, he kissed me again. Gently, he glided off my lips.

My thoughts screamed in jubilation; he is sincere. I do want to spend the rest of my life with him. I don't care if anybody approves. I want him.

"Hi back. I missed you too. I was mad at you for not calling; I waited all week. Each day I thought you would call, and each day you didn't, became miserable. My," Rudy interrupted.

"I apologize," A kiss on my cheek. "I'm sorry," A kiss on my forehead. "Forgive me, please," Our lips met again.

In an instant, we were French kissing. I became mesmerized. Rudy eased off, insisting, "Say you forgive me. I have to hear you say it."

"I forgive you," I said breathlessly.

"Yee-ah! Let's go have some fun at the Silly Goose."

Clayton interrupted his thoughts, "Little angel, Jason's advice was correct. Oh, but to be young. Seldom does youth listen to advise. Our youthful ears do not want to comprehend the adult passage. Everybody travels the inexperienced road. As time catches up, we become experienced. Our journey on the road of life hopefully ends with only a few potholes. The repaired potholes are good life experiences; if we go around the potholes, nothing is learned. The rut of life is ending up in the potholes. Some poor souls never get out of the rut, missing the beauty of life altogether.

You, little angel, never experienced life. Don't be concerned. Your soul will live again. Next time you will not suffer from the misdeeds of a troubled adult. You will get a chance at life, and it will be marvelous for you. You'll have the right blend of compassion and knowledge to make your life grand."

Clayton caressed the baby angel for a moment, and the little one cooed approvingly. "But I need to continue with Andrea's saga. I must understand why her reasoning was so misguided, why she went to the edge of the oblivion crypt. She knew the consequences.

Why?"

TWENTY
The Silly Goose

While driving toward the club, I asked, "When do I meet your mother? After all your preparation, I think it should be soon."

"Yes. We will meet mother tomorrow, at three o'clock." Pensive Rudy continued, "I don't want to startle you, but she is into readings. For as long as I can remember, she has been doing readings. She wants to do your reading as soon as you get there. It has to get started at three, sharp."

"Readings? I don't get it. Why does she want to read me a book? What kind of book?"

Rudy laughed.

I asked, "What's so funny?"

"Not a book reading, a tarot reading."

"O-o-o-o. I've never done that, and I don't know anybody who has either. What do I wear? What do I say? Are you going to be with me?"

"Don't hassle over it. I don't want to talk about it anymore. It brings back bad memories of the past week. I want to forget about it. I just want to have fun tonight."

For the first time being around Rudy, I felt sadness. I could not imagine what this meant. Without saying a word, I reached for his hand and touched it soothingly. He tenderly took my hand and kissed it gently.

"Okay, maybe we will talk later," He conceded.

Rudy started, channel surfing the radio, as he lit up a smoke. "By the way, you look sensational."

My complexion turned pink, and I suddenly became warm, my usual reaction when he complimented me. All I could muster was thanks, and I hoped he didn't notice my embarrassment. Strangest reaction as I never blushed when others complimented me.

Arriving at the Silly Goose, parking the car, I got ready to turn off the car.

Rudy immediately said, "Don't open the door. I'll come around."

Turning crimson again, I hoped Rudy would not think this was my natural look.

"Okay. If you want."

"Yes. I want."

Before he got out of the car, he reached over and kissed me gently on the lips.

As he came around to my side of the car, I stared at him through the windshield. He was gorgeous.

Opening the door, he extended his arm, and I gently took his hand, walking toward the building hand in hand.

Reaching the entrance, Rudy stepped forward, opening the door. A small line, about six people, were in front—a woman stood by a podium asking for identification.

I looked at Rudy and whispered, "I didn't know we were going to be carded. I'm not twenty-one."

"Don't worry about it," Rudy said, as he smiled.

Approaching the woman, Rudy touted, "Hey, Tootsie, you, beautiful sword. What's gleaming?"

Rudy hugged her. Bending slightly, he kissed her on the cheek.

Reciprocating his hug and kiss, the petite, dark-haired viraginous woman shouted with glee, "Rudy. Where have you been? I can't remember the last time you were here. How is Ms. Julia?"

"Away from you, and she's still the emperor."

Tootsie laughed.

"You better show me some respect. Now get in here before I card you or worst, deny you entry." Laughing robustly, she said, "Wait. You've got that spell on me. Put your hand out. You know nobody gets in without being stamped."

Looking at me, "You too, Love. Your hand." In a flash, she stamped my hand too. Walking away, I glanced at my hand,
imprinted a comical goose with flapping wings and a wide-eyed surprised look.

We stepped down into the central area of the lounge.

"Where do you want to sit?" Rudy asked.

"Let's sit near the door until Maggie arrives. She isn't twenty-one either. She'll need your help getting in."

We walked toward the bar area. Reaching for the barstools, Rudy asked, "What do you want to drink?"

"I'm not sure. I guess, anything uncola."

"That's right. I forgot," Rudy tapped his forehead. "You should try getting wild. Order a cola, how about it?" Rudy said jokingly.

I stuck my tongue out at him, saying, "I hate cola."

Rudy laughed as he gestured for the bartender.

He ordered. "We'll have a draft and a cherry beer."

"What's a cherry beer?"

"You'll see."

Looking at the entrance, I saw Maggie standing in line. We waved at her as Maggie saw us and waved back.

"Marvelous. I'll go over there as soon as we get our drinks."

No sooner did he say that, when the bartender appeared with the drinks.

Vivaciously Rudy said, "Hey, K doll. What's rising?" He laughed at his remark.

Equally as spirited, the bartender blew a kiss toward Rudy, saying, "You Bitch."

Making a catching motion, Rudy smacked his butt with the imaginary kiss.

The bartender said, "I'm still waiting for you to come over, you hussy. The suds are on me."

"Thanks, but I'm worth more than two brews."

"Prove it, Sweetheart."

Laughing hysterically, Rudy said, "Maybe someday." "You tease. Oops, getting busy, gotta go before I get fired. Then I'll never become a Barbie."

Rudy blew a kiss to him. The bartender encircled his lips with his tongue, winked, and roguishly giggled.

"It appears you've been here before," I commented. Adding, "Quite often."

"Not really. Tootsie is part-owner. Since I was a toddler, she's known my mother and has readings done once a month, without fail, by Ms. Julia. More

often, if business slows down.

Before this place opened, they needed help. My mother volunteered me. I helped with just about everything, including hiring—what a crazy time. I had a blast too. I've known Chris for a long time. He's a super bartender. I recommended him for the job."

Rudy slid off the barstool, ready to get Maggie.

"Wait. Before you go, get Maggie. What's a K doll?"

"The short version, a transgender."

Giggling, "That explains your antics."

Rudy hugged me quickly and left to get Maggie.

Sipping the drink, I noticed a cherry at the bottom of the glass. Drinking more of the liquid, I finally realized it was a non-alcoholic beer, laughed to myself, said out loud, "Cherry beer. I get it!"

Rudy grabbed my waist, exclaimed, "Here we are. We better find a table; otherwise, we'll be at the bar the rest of the night."

"Maggie. What took you so long?"

Maggie said, "Couldn't find a happy top. It doesn't matter now. This is great."

Rudy picked up his glass, saying, "This way."

As I stood, I felt a strange sensation on my buttocks. I immediately turned around. Rudy stood behind, giggling shamelessly.

"What are you doing?"

"I goosed you. I wanted to be the first. Wait until you get on the dance floor."

"Now I understand the warning," Maggie said.

"What warning?" Rudy asked. Sage said, "Girls should not wear a skirt or a dress to this place."

We all laughed as Rudy escorted us to a table. Rudy pulled out a chair saying, "Sage." Then pulled out another chair, "Maggie."

"Thanks. You're so kind." Maggie said.

"Yeah. What did I tell you?"

Rudy pulled out his chair and sat between us, asked Maggie, "What would you like to drink?"

"I'll have whatever you're drinking."

Rudy gestured to the waitress at the bar, pointed at his glass raised two fingers. The waitress acknowledged him.

Maggie asked, "Why are you drinking a cherry beer?"

Surprised by her remark, I asked, "How do you know it's a cherry beer?"

"I've been around."

"Are you going out without me? I told Rudy to order me anything uncola. Funny, cherry beer."

All of us laughed as the waitress arrived with the drinks. Rudy gulped his beer and handed the empty glass to the waitress. She gave him a full glass and put a foaming glass in front of Maggie.

"Thanks. Put it on my tab." Rudy quipped.

As she left, the waitress winked, saying, "Gotcha."

"The music montage is going to start soon. That's the best part of this place. Of course, I thought of it." Rudy gleamed proudly.

"What is the music montage?" I asked.

"For about an hour, the DJ plays different music, a few bars or so. That's when you have to look out—anything goes."

"Like being goosed?" Maggie asked.

"Yea."

"Did you think of that too?" Maggie continued.

"Not really, that kind of happened. It's turned out to be an interesting and fun idea. This place gets a lot of repeat partiers. It's incredible. Once goosed, it seems to start a chain reaction. Like yawning. You'll see."

I shouted, "I think I see Buster?"

94

"Where?" Maggie asked, looking around.

"Over there. Near the bar."

Maggie and Rudy looked as I pointed toward the middle of the bar.

"Sure is," Rudy confirmed. He stood, said, "I'll go ask him to come join us."

As he made his way into the dim-lit room, a hand reached out and goosed him. Maggie and I looked at each other and giggled unmercifully. "I'm glad we got the warning," Maggie said.

"Me too. Quick, what do you think of Rudy now?"

"I guess I was wrong. If you're happy, I'm happy for you. How does he know so much about this place?"

"He knows the owner," I hurriedly answered. Taking a deep breath, I continued, "I'm supposed to meet his mother tomorrow. She sounds weird. She wants to do a tarot reading on me."

"Cool." Maggie, sanctioned. Taking a sip from the chilly beer, she continued, "Be your sensible self; she'll have to like you."

"I'll try. I want her to like me. Rudy apologized for not calling. Isn't he cool?"

Rudy and Buster approached the table. Maggie and I shouted, "Hey, Buster."

"A cherry beer?" Buster asked.

"Rudy, being funny." I finished the drink said, "The real stuff, please."

We laughed as Rudy signaled for the waitress.

Rudy asked, "Anybody else, ready for another?"

"Sure, why not? Have ta get ready for the montage." Buster said as he emptied his half glass.

"I'm fine," Maggie said.

"Three regular drafts," Rudy ordered.

They all looked at me. I punched Rudy on the arm as I shouted, "He was kidding."

"Don't get violent, get even. Give him a surprise goose," Buster said.

All of us laughed exuberantly. The waitress came back with the order in no time. She put the full glasses down and picked up the empties.

Picking up my glass, she asked, "Don't you want the cherry, Love? It's better than the beer."

Everybody exclaimed, "He was kidding." Grasping the glass, I briskly guzzled the cherry, chewed, and swallowed at the same time.

Everybody applauded, chanting, "Woof-woof-woof! Way to go." I, too, applauded.

Buster lifted his glass, "A toast. To the good times. Remember them always."

For some reason, this did not sound like Buster.

"I'll drink to that," Maggie said, taking a quick sip, asked, "Why so somber?"

"I'm going to be leaving soon."

"Where are you going?" Maggie asked.

"I'm moving to Alaska."

We all said, "Alaska?"

Continuing her query, Maggie asked, "Why are you moving to Alaska?"

"I think it's the farthest place from here." Then he looked at Maggie, "I've heard people mine their own business too."

Maggie made a comical face saying, "O-o-o-o."

"Are you in trouble or thinking of doing something stupid, Buster?" I asked.

Maggie said, "We're your friends. If you need help, tell us."

Buster drank some of his beer. Put the glass down, looked at it, took a deep breath, slowly said, "I'm in love."

Rudy looked at me. He took my hand tenderly and squeezed it.

"That's the ultimate. Did you meet on the internet? Is she from Alaska? Is she a mail order bride?" I asked.

Smirking, Maggie said, "Yeah, or is she missing the 's'?"

Defensively Buster stated, "She is not, a he."

"Love is not a crime. Why do you sound like a criminal?" I asked.

"I don't want you guys to laugh, okay?"

"Love is not a joke, Buster. It's okay." I said.

Buster blurted out, "I'm in love with my cousin."

We looked at each other, bewildered.

Finally, I said, "That's a joke, right?"

Buster stated, "It just happened. I didn't know she was my cousin. One day I came home, and this beautiful vision sat on the couch. I introduced myself.

We had instant karma, talked and laughed like we had known each other always. Then I kissed her, and she kissed me back–electrifying. I have never felt such sparks–such love. I don't care what anyone thinks. My love for her s unconditional. In Alaska, we can be together. No one will care."

"When did you find out she was your cousin?" Maggie asked.

"Later that evening. I asked my parents how they knew Rhonda. Mother said, 'She's your cousin.' I was floored, numbed. Mom explained something

about a family riff; it happened before I was born, something about her older brother. I never heard anything about him, and I haven't even met him; I stopped listening. I could see mom's lips move, but I could not hear the words. All I could think about was my love for Rhonda. That's when I made up my mind. I talked to Rhonda, and she didn't know we were

cousins either. She feels about me the same way. So we started making plans. I told her, as soon as I paid off my Van, we are Alaska bound."

"Is she old or ugly or what?" Maggie asked.

"No, Maggie. We are about the same age. She's eighteen and knock-out beautiful." Buster said with conviction.

Maggie stated with her usual confidence, "You know, if you have kids, they'll be morons. Retards, you idiot. It's not natural."

"I don't care. We won't have kids. I'll put that on my list."

Pulling out a piece of paper and a pen, Buster wrote something

"What's that?" Maggie asked.

"It's my plans before we leave. I just added vasectomy. I will do anything for our love."

"You're crazy, and she's just as demented to go along with this crazy love," Retorted Maggie.

Buster tenderly said, "Come on, Maggie, I can't help it. It just happened. What do you two think?" Looking at Rudy and me.

"I'm with Maggie. You don't fall in love with your cousin, Buster. You have fun and love your cousin but not fall in love," I said.

Rudy said, "I don't know, man. But you're going to need lots of help to pull it off." Rudy grabbed a charm he had around his neck, unclasped it, saying, "Here. Take this. It always brought luck. You're going to need it a lot more than me."

Buster took the charm. Put it around his neck, saying, "Thanks. I never expected this." His voice started to quiver. He took a sip from the beer, cleared his throat. He said, "This is probably the last time we will be together."

We had never seen this sentimental side of Buster. He always joked around. Seeing him like this was unusual and unnatural for him.

"You sure know how to bring down a party," Maggie said, visibly shaken.

At that moment, a loud voice said, "Okay, goslings, are you ready to get goosed?" Characteristic cries of a goose blasted throughout the lounge.

Buster leaped up shouted, "Honk, honk. The montage." He looked at Maggie, gestured toward the dance floor. "For old times." Putting out his hand.

Maggie sprung up, slapped him five. "Honk, honk. Let's dance."

They went towards the dance floor. Buster shouting, "Honk, honk!"

"What a nut," Rudy said.

As we watched them trot to the dance floor, Buster flapped his arms all the way and shouting honk-honk, honk-honk.

"Wanna join them?" Rudy asked seductively, kissing my hand.

"Sure. First, I'd like to say that it was nice of you to give Buster your charm."

"I've got you. I don't need it anymore. You are my lucky charm now." Rudy took my hand and caressed his face. We gently kissed.

For the first time, I did not blush, and for the first time, I initiated a kiss. We stood to go to the dance floor. Rudy led me to the already crowded dance area. Before he turned around, I goosed him.

"Hey, what was that?"

"I wanted to be the first."

We laughed and started to dance.

After forty-five minutes of nonstop dancing, I gasped, "Let's sit."

Rudy acknowledged. We walked back to the table, breathing heavily. I picked up the glass and took a big swallow of beer, "Yuk. This beer is warm."

Rudy gestured to the waitress, ordering four more beers. The waitress swiftly brought fresh beer and cleared the stale glasses.

I drank from the fresh liquid, satisfying my thirst and breathing normally; I said, "That was a riot. I loved it."

"Yeah, it's a scream, or should I say a honker?"

Laughing, we see Buster and Maggie make their way to the table too. They were also breathing heavily. Grabbing their schooners, guzzled without saying a word.

"I can't believe it. I thought we were going to make it until the end."

Maggie said, gasping for air and wiping the sweat from her brow.

"No way. The DJ keeps playing as long as there is a crowd on the floor. The music can go on for hours." Rudy said.

"Wo-o-o-o, what an event," Maggie exclaimed. She took another drink, finally catching her breath.

Buster took a long sip, wiped the beer mustache and the rest of his sweaty face with the tiny bar napkin.

"I forgot to mention something else. I'm changing my name when I get to Alaska."

"Okay. I'm ready, to what?" Maggie asked.

"Gomez," Buster said seriously.

"Where did you come up with a name like that?" Maggie scolded him.

"A movie I liked."

"I guess it's better than Fester," Maggie said.

Rudy and I chuckled at her comment.

"Maggie. You're terrible." I said.

"What? It's a goofy name." Looking at Buster, Maggie sincerely said, "You take that off your list. No, name change, okay?"

"I'll think about it."

Buster finished his beer, scooted the chair out, stood, and said, "It's been fun. I hate to leave, but I have arrangements to make. I wanted a last look at the old stomping grounds; it's not the same. I miss Rhonda at my side. That's what I had to know. If you guys don't see me around, come to Alaska."

Maggie stood, giving Buster a tight hug saying, "Tons of luck. You, insane Loon."

I also stood and hugged him, saying, "Think about this some more, will you? But if you go through with it, peace and love."

"The parties won't be the same, man." Rudy shook Buster's hand.

Buster hugged him, saying, "Buy some rotgut now and then and think of me. Thanks for the charm; I hope it still has luck."

We smiled as Buster walked away. That night was the last time we saw Buster.

Looking at her mother, Sage stopped telling the story asked, "I know what Buster did was morally wrong. Does this mean he's going to hell?"

Andrea responded, "There is no hell. If Buster gets his trinity, his spirit energy will continue. If not, his energy will eventually die in the oblivion crypt."

Sage thought for a moment, softly said, "I hope he gets his trinity."

She continued her story of unconditional love.

"We left the club shortly after Buster departed.

"I don't feel like dancing anymore. I'm outta here." Maggie said.

"Yeah. I'm not in a partying mood either. Besides, I have to get my beauty sleep for tomorrow."

Maggie went her way, and I drove Rudy home.

"Don't be late. Three o'clock sharp." Rudy said as I left him on the curb.

Driving home, I started thinking of Rudy's remark that he had to prepare her.

Driving onto the driveway, parked, and slowly walked to my room, obsessively thought, prepare her for what?

Setting the alarm to make sure I would not oversleep, my wonderment slowly faded as I blurred into a slumber.

TWENTY-ONE
Ms. Julia

Arriving at Rudy's house, he was outside waiting for me. I parked the car. He opened the car door. Stepping out, he hugged and kissed me.

"Mother is waiting. I'm glad you're early."

We walked toward the house holding hands.

Approaching the entry, Rudy said, "You look sensational. Don't worry about anything. I love you. Nobody can change that, not even mother."

He gave me another quick kiss before opening the door.

From the entrance, we walked to the left into the living room. The sparsely decorated room had a rust-brown early American sofa against one wall—a television across the sofa and a large window on another wall with thick white curtains. The outside light barely seeped through. There were no pictures–not family life, still life, nothing. The milky white walls bare except for decoration over the sofa. It appeared to be a cross I didn't recognize. Thinking, I must ask Rudy about that decoration over the sofa.

I saw a diminutive woman with henna colored hair, didn't fit in with the rest of the family. I couldn't tell how old she was. She looked younger than Rudy. Whatever she used to obtain her youthful looks, it worked!

Arthur was probably in his mid-sixties, a handsome man despite the beer gut. His slightly receding hairline had remnants of dark brown hair. Not as mesmerizing as Rudy's, his dark eyes had a sparkle of naughtiness, an instantly likable man.

Rudy started the introductions.

"Mother, Arthur, this is Sage. Sage, this is Arthur and Julia."

Arthur commented in one breath, "Glad to meet you. No wonder Rudy's been a lunatic; you're a vision. She's very pleasant on the eyes' Son, way to go."

Before I said anything, Julia interrupted, "Enough with the introductions, call me Ms. Julia. Everybody does. Welcome to our home. Come with me."

Rudy reassured me, "It's okay. I'll be here. Mother is anxious to start the reading. It has to start at three o'clock sharp. It won't take long."

Ms. Julia said, "Don't be nervous, child, we are going to have a girl talk.."

Ms. Julia gently took hold of my arm, directed me toward a corridor, said, "This is the first time Rudy has brought a girlfriend over. I'm so excited," She turned around, gruffly said, "Okay, boys, don't disturb us."

"We know the routine, Ms. Julia," Arthur said, softly laughing. Rudy winked, comforting me slightly.

We walked the corridor toward the back of the house—the hallway, also empty of decorations. Only the sounds of our footsteps broke the silence, the emptiness, like walking the corridors of a mausoleum.

Ms. Julia's floor-length, black skirt gave her the illusion of floating. It was sort of cool.

Ms. Julia opened the door to a cold room with antique furnishings, and velvet cloth spewed about—gave it warmth. A heavy scent of incense added excitement. I couldn't ascertain the aroma, like entering a Jewish bakery, pleasant exotic smells that instantly vitalize. It intrigued me.

Ms. Julia directed me to sit by the table in the middle of the room.

She went to the only window, closed the shade, and drew the curtains shut.

In the dark, one could still see shadows. The shadowy figure of

Ms. Julia walked to a credenza, emanating drawers' sounds opening and closing. A dancing match flame lit a candelabrum atop the credenza. Ms. Julia made her way toward me, now wearing a beautiful silk purple shawl.

In one hand, she carried two white candles, and in the other, a little wooden box made of strange-looking wood, maybe mahogany or teak. It was a dark shiny wood but very porous. If I didn't know better, I'd say it was a sponge wood—glistening dark sponge wood.

Opening the box, she took out another candle. Handing me a match, she instructed me to light the candle from the box first, light the two candles with the original, and place the candles in a triangular formation between us.

"I want you to rid yourself of all thoughts. Concentrate on the flames. Let your energies be one with the candles. Dance with the flames. Cleanse your thoughts."

Ms. Julia chanted while taking a small bundle from the box, carefully placed between us. Setting the wooden box at the edge of the table, she opened the white silk cloth bundle, revealing the tarot cards.

She started shuffling the cards religiously. Hypnotically, she placed the cards between us, instructed me to cut the deck right to left, and make three stacks—Ms. Julia then put the deck together left to right.

"I'm going to arrange a spread called a Celtic cross. It will be ten cards in a cross pattern. I'll let you know what each card represents. After I deal all the cards, the reading will start."

As she flipped a card, she said, "The first card is the cover. It is strength, reversed. The second card is your crossing. It is the queen of cups, reversed. The third card is your foundation. It is the queen of wands, reversed. The fourth card is what has passed. It is the tower, reversed. The fifth card is what may come to pass. It is the two of swords, reversed. The sixth card is what you must face. It is the nine of wands, reversed. The seventh card is what you feel. It is the two of pentacles, reversed. The eighth card is what others think. It is the ten of cups, reversed. The ninth card is what you want. It is the star, reversed. The tenth card is the resolution. It is the king of cups, reversed." Ms. Julia paused, breathed laboriously.

She said, "In thirty years, I have never seen a spread where all the cards are reversed—the odds of this happening baffle the imagination; the chances of the sun exploding are better than seeing a spread like this.

Ms. Julia paused again rubbed her temples.

"I cannot go on. I must meditate."

She stared at the cards, like visitors at the zoo during feeding time, unprepared, horrified but unable to stop staring. She reached for the box, frantically searched for something.

"Here it is, wear this staurolite necklace, from this moment on, do not take it off. Now, I must be alone. Tell Rudy and Arthur I must meditate."

"What's the big deal? Am I going to die? Is something tragic going to happen to someone I know? My Dad?" I began to feel frightened.

Cautiously Ms. Julia said, "No, no, no. I have never seen a spread like this. I have lost my concentration—I'm so embarrassed. We will have to do a reading
another time. Now, please, I must meditate."

The instant Ms. Julia turned the last card, her effervescent mood turned somber. I left the room with a chilly, eerie feeling.

Entering the living room, Rudy said, "See, it's over, that wasn't so bad?"

"She didn't finish the reading. Something about having to meditate right now. She gave me this necklace."

"That's peculiar. But, you never know with Ms. Julia. She is into the cards. When she starts to meditate, we never know how long she's going to be in there. Come, let's go to my apartment. We need to talk."

I followed Rudy outside to another entrance. He led me to some stairs that were on the side of the house. We went up ten steps. Entering his apartment, the smell of the incense lingered.

"I don't notice the smell much except when Mother is in her room."

He turned on a lamp, like a night light, the glow did not shed much light. Two small round windows with black curtains limited the access to natural light. The room was lit, like a theater before the movie begins.

A small white sofa against one wall. On the opposite wall, a bare, long-legged table, with a small TV on it. The hanging over the couch—precisely like the one downstairs.

"Is that a cross? I have never seen one like that," I asked.

"It's an Ankh, an Egyptian cross. It has several meanings. One means life. Someday I'll tell you a second meaning. Would you like something to drink? All I have is beer. Oh, water too."

"Water, please."

Rudy went to the kitchenette, which was the adjacent room. A half-wall, the only partition. A small refrigerator, a two-burner stove, without an oven, and a bar sink made up the kitchen. He came back with a bottle of beer and a bottle of water. He uncapped the water, handed it to me, uncapped the other, and he took a long swallow. We sat on the couch.

"We have to talk."

"What's on your mind?"

Enthusiastic Rudy said, "One of my professors has left for Europe. He received a grant to study European architecture. If the grant holds out, he'll be gone for about a year, maybe more. He's single and needed someone to house sit. Last week he asked me. I had to act fast before somebody else jumped on it—I told him yes. Imagine a place of our own, rent-free. We can start knowing each other, nurturing each other now."

Rudy paused, looked at my astonishment.

He continued, "I know last week was difficult. I told mother about you, and that I was moving out. She didn't take the news well. She'll get over it. It's us now; let's move in together. What do you say?"

Startled by the question, I paused before responding. "I didn't expect this. Is your mother going to hate me? She'll think I put you up to this. She'll blame me for losing her son. You still have to meet my Dad. What if he doesn't approve?"

He put his right index finger on my lips, said, "Shhh. Don't ask questions. You're all I think about, I know it's all happening fast, but we should grab it instead of letting go. If you want, I'll meet your Dad tomorrow. As for my mother, she doesn't hate anyone, least of all my true love. You're the center of my universe now. I don't care what anybody else thinks. Our destiny is to become one."

He came closer and kissed me like never before. His intense energy lulled my apprehensions, putting me on a different level of passion, and I wanted more.

He backed off dauntless, said, "Please answer yes."

I couldn't resist. "Yes. But, I have to tell Dad. I'm sure he'll understand. When do we move in?"

"Anytime, Professor Lynn departed last Friday. I'm going to move my things this week. You can join me anytime. The sooner, the better." "First things first. My Dad. I won't do anything until I tell him."

"I understand." Rudy kissed me again, reinforcing the idea. He continued, "Since mother is meditating, no use hanging around here. Dad doesn't get involved much. He figures I'm old enough to be on my own. Would you like to check out our new place? Doesn't that sound great? Our place."

"Sure, let's go."

We went back downstairs. Found Arthur in the living room watching TV and drinking a beer.

I took my purse, saying, "It was very nice meeting you. Please tell Ms. Julia we'll have to get together again soon."

Nonchalantly Arthur stated, "You're nice. Hell, when she gets this way, she's even too spooky for me. And I've been around this for a long time."

Looking at Rudy, he said, "It's about time, boy, I was getting worried about you. But you picked a beauty."

Smiling, Rudy said, "I'm a late bloomer, take after the old man."

Arthur gave Rudy a pretend punch on his left arm. They both laughed.

Rudy and I departed.

I never saw Arthur and Ms. Julia again.

TWENTY-TWO
The House

With the sun giving way to the moon, we arrived at the house in Oak Park.

"Are you sure this is the house?"

"I've been here before. Of course, I'm sure."

"This is the Heurtley House. We can't go in there."

Grinning, Rudy said, "I know this is the Heurtley House. And yes we, can." He dangled a set of keys, saying, "I've got the keys; this will be our house for at least a year. Wait until you see the inside. You won't want to leave. The energy that erupts from here is incredible."

Still, in awe, I exclaimed, "How could Professor Lynn leave this in your care—this is a huge responsibility? This the Heurtley House. History. You better get your charm back from Buster; this has to be supernatural luck."

Rudy chuckled. "You are my lucky charm now. Stop asking questions. Enjoy the moment. The house is architectural history. Feel it around us. The living room is spectacular. That's the room I want you to experience first."

Parking the car, I slowly got out in a zombie-like state. All I could do was follow Rudy. I became captivated before realizing we were in the living room. In the background, I faintly heard a voice.

"Are you okay?" Rudy asked as he poked my shoulder.

"Uhuh," I said, returning to reality

"Is this stupendous or what?"

"Stupendous or what," I echoed.

The sunburst fireplace drew my attention. Though it did not have a crackling fire, you could feel the energy, sensational. The essence of the imaginary heat burst out, like a welder's torch.

"Lay on the floor and look at the ceiling," Rudy whispered as if not to wake anybody, and we laid side by side.

"Omigod," A breathtaking scene.

The ceiling, encrusted by two trapezoid shapes of dark wood, dramatic stained-glass skylights, embodied the center. Golden yellows and black made the motif. Displaying triangles at one point, but a continuous stare revealed winglike forms were soaring above in tranquillity. I became hypnotized by the dazzling beauty and the energy, like the finale of a fireworks display.

We laid there for hours in silence. The tranquillity epitomized heaven on earth.

"I must tell, Dad. Then I can move in. I know he will approve. Wait until Maggie sees this place. She'll be as mesmerized. I know it.

We'll have to have tons of parties. Maybe do what Monica and Vinney do, a free-for-all. Except for no writings on the walls. This place is too beautiful; we have to share it."

Rudy became annoyed, said, "This will be our place. Not to be shared with too many people. The energy in this room is harmonic; we won't break up that harmony. This house is our sanctuary, a place to regain balance after battling the world. I will not jeopardize this peaceful spirit."

He gently kissed me, and his temperament became loving again, conceding, "Okay, maybe one party, close friends only."

It didn't matter; whatever he said, I condoned. We left the house euphoric.

TWENTY-THREE
Telling Dad

Running into the house, I shouted, "Dad. Where are you?" Scarcely heard his response.

"In the study."

I ran toward the study, found Dad reading in his favorite chair.

"Dad. When can you meet Rudy?"

"Greetings to you too. What's the big hurry?" Jason paused, compassionately asked, "Are you pregnant?"

As I walked closer, I hugged him said, "Hi. No, I'm not pregnant. There is no big hurry. I want you to meet cause we're moving in together."

"What? How long have you been planning this? You just met, now you're moving together?"

Catching his breath, calming down, he said, "I know I can't forbid you from moving out, and by the sound of it, I can't change your mind. Can I?"

"Dad. What happened to the old saying, you haven't lost a daughter; you've gained a son?"

"That's a bunch of crap! Some old wives' tale, made up by some old couple who had an ugly daughter on the verge of being an old maid. That crappy saying doesn't apply today, probably never did. Once a daughter becomes a mother, it's never the same. Gained a son, phooey!"

His response surprised me.

"Dad, you sound hostile. I've never heard you like this."

Jason paused, calmly said, "You've never come home telling me you're moving out. I knew this moment had to come sooner or later. When do we meet? I'll be civil, don't expect much more."

"Is tomorrow night about seven, all right?" I asked childlike.

"That's fine," He managed to say, having to stop to regain control; he continued, "When do you plan on moving?

"This weekend, all I need is my clothes and stuff."

Startled again, Jason began pacing, firing questions, "Are you still going to school? What about when you start traveling? Is he going to accept your traveling around the world without him? Is he going to be loyal to you? You deserve loyalty. Trust. What about marriage? Has he asked you to marry him? Please don't say you're going to get married. I know we've had our new adult old adult talk, but you're too young for marriage Sweet Basil. Travel, enjoy your career. Experience and see different cultures. First, love life before you love someone."

"Yes, I'm going to school. I'm not worrying about anything else. I'm living for the moment. You've taught me to plan things out, be cautious— question everything. I'm tired of that. I want to be spontaneous. I want to experience it all now." I responded confidently.

Looking down, then at his daughter, Jason sternly but softly said, "You're talking about your future, not a picnic. Spontaneity is okay when you're at the mall. Spontaneity is not okay when you move out and start to share your life with someone. Remember, choice or chance: Choice is planning. Chance is random. In the long run, planned experiences are better than random ones. Choice makes more sense, doesn't it?"

"Yes, but I'm not alone. Rudy's love is sincere. See him through my eyes, Daddy. We are going to make it. I promise you this; we'll live together for a year, then we'll get married. My choice. Be happy for me."

"You have left me no choice, Sweet Basil. Don't ever forget; I love you. Unconditionally. Always."

Sage stopped telling her story.

"Mother. Dad truly loved me. I've known it all my life but never thought about it. I took his love for granted because he was always there. I think I let him down. I know I took advantage of him at times, never on serious things. I think he knew, and he let me go for it anyway. Now he's alone. Is he going to be okay?"

Remembering Jason, Andrea softly said, "Knowing your Dad, he'll be fine."

"Great. Now I don't feel so bad." Sage continued, "Dad and I had excellent talks. When it came to our talks, Dad always had answers. I'll miss them." Then added, "But my love turned to Rudy. I must continue."

Andrea observed her daughter thinking she is young, foolish, and naive. Maybe she will understand my side of unconditional love. Is there hope?

Andrea thought of the soothing white light to help her maintain the harmony in the catacomb.

Clayton sobbed. "Why didn't she stop this madness? Hope? She should have stopped!"

He hugged the little angel, trying to understand the anguish inside his soul. He had never known this much anguish in the afterlife. Why weren't the catacombs filtering out his grief? Most of all, he became more adamant about trying to comprehend Andrea's persistence.

TWENTY-FOUR
Rudy and Jason

The door chime broke the silence of the house. I knew it had to be Rudy. The closer I walked to the door, the more nervous I became. I wanted Dad to like Rudy so bad my insides ached. It would be a fairytale if Dad approved. Opening the door and giving me a quick kiss, Rudy said, "Hi precious."

I took him through the dining room, the family room then to the study. Jason stood as we approached.

"Dad, I'd like you to meet Rudy. Rudy, this is my dad, Jason."

"Pleasure to meet you."

"Pleasure is mine, Dad." Self-assured, Rudy continued, "Before you make any judgment, I want you to know I truly love your daughter. We are meant to be together."

Jason took a deep breath, "Rudy, would you like anything to drink?"

"Beer's okay."

"Import or domestic?"

"Domestic, of course."

Jason walked to the mini-bar, opened the refrigerator, grabbed a beer, poured half the libation then handed Rudy the glass and bottle. He poured himself a cognac, took a sip, savored the smooth liquid.

"Meant to be, huh? Have you ever done this before—loved someone this quick?"

"I have never felt this way about anyone. I never will. We will be together always," Rudy responded emphatically.

Jason immediately said, "Always is a long time. I'd be pleased if you made one year, only because Sage wants it so bad. You are not the only one who loves her. I prefer she start her career before she ventured into this stage of life."

Jason looked at his daughter with love and concern, saying, "My preference has nothing to do with it now."

He then turned to Rudy, continued, "I wanted you to know that."

Still cocked with self-assurance, Rudy said, "Thanks, Dad. I'll remember that. I want her to start her career too; I'm not the problem, I'm the solution."

Jason took another sip of cognac. Calmly asked, "Do you play billiards?"

"Sure." Rudy said blandly.

"Better warn you, Dad is a master pool player."

Jason smiled, "Just a friendly game. Let's go to my lounge."

From the study, we walked back to the foyer, to the spiraling stairs. We went down to Dad's lounge. Decorative bar lights and beer signs lighted the room.

"Wait here," Jason commanded at the bottom of the stairs. Walking across the room, he turned up the dim light over the pool table, pointed to a wall, "The sticks. Do you want to go first or lag?

Boldly Rudy said, "Lag."

I kissed Rudy on the cheek. "I don't want to see the massacre. I'll be at the bar setting up refreshments and sandwiches. Good luck," Winking at Rudy, "You'll need it.

Rudy walked to the rack and took a stick. Jason took his from the pool table and chalked up.

"Whenever you're ready," Jason said.

Rudy hit the ball. Jason followed, winning the lag.

"Eightball. Rack'em up."

Arrogantly Rudy set up the balls.

Jason slammed the triangular formation, breaking the silence of the table with a rumble. The balls scattered explosively in all directions. Two balls went into the pockets, the twelve in the right corner, the three in the left-center. Intensely looking over the table, Jason patiently waited for the splash

of color to trickle to a halt.

The cueball stopped near the foot spot, five and seven positioned near the eft corner pocket, four near the right corner pocket, six near the center, neighbored to the left by the eightball. The one ball had parked between the foot string and center. The two sat at the head of the table between the center string and head string.

Jason announced, "Solids."

Shooting at the seven, it softly dropped in the left corner pocket, the cue-ball came off the end rail, perfect set-up for the five-ball.

Jason struck the five-ball into the left corner pocket. The solid white ball hit the left rail, rolling between the foot string and the center string. A hard hit, shot the cue-ball toward the four, pocketing the ball in the right corner pocket. The deadly white sphere came off the end rail, aiming for the table's head, kicked the nine out of the line of fire, cleared a shot for the two-ball.

The cue ball stopped about six inches from the center string. Striking the cue-ball, it hit the two forcefully into the right corner pocket at the head of the table. The cue-ball banked off the headrail. Rolling, rolling, rolling then stopped about twelve inches from the left-center pocket.

Jason slowly chalked up. In deep concentration, he prepared to strike the one ball.

A tapping sound distracted him for a moment. Looking toward the sound, he saw Rudy nonchalantly tapping his fingers on the bar.

Jason struck the one ball dead center, leaving the cue ball in the perfect line-up for the six– into the right corner.

Slowly walking around the table, he took a sip of cognac and glanced at Rudy. Still tapping his fingers, Jason smiled, announcing the final shot, "Eight, left corner pocket."

Bringing the stick down, he firmly sent the eight ball into the called pocket.

Rudy applauded, whistled, then yelled, "Ye-e-ah maestro."

Coming back with sandwiches, dip, and corn chips, I said, "Warned you he was good."

Rudy put the stick on the table, hastily made his way toward Jason, hugging him, saying, "Magnificent, Dad. I've never seen anybody play like that. I'll have to play more often now."

At that moment, Jason sensed forced enthusiasm from Rudy.

Rudy asked, "Do you play Sage?" "Not as well as Dad. I can't get as intense. Maybe that's my problem."

Jason left his stick on the table, picked up Rudy's, and placed it on the rack where it belonged.

Walking toward the sandwiches, Jason said, "You don't need intense; you
do need a small amount of concentration." He winked cheerfully at me and took a bite of the sandwich.

"I play for fun, not necessarily to win."

"That's your second problem; we play to win."

Rudy picked up a sandwich and took a bite.

"This is very tasty. Did you make it?"

"I did. Using an old family recipe, my mother improved. She was a great cook."

Jason quickly corrected her declaring, "Chef. Your mother was a great Chef. Her love for the culinary arts, passion for life, and hard work afforded her the respect from her peers and the title Chef."

"Sorry, Dad. I know that. I didn't think it mattered."

"It matters."

Rudy instantly said, "That's the kind of passion I want."

Clearing his throat, taking a sip from his freshly poured cognac, Jason tenderly and softly said, "I wish I could make it happen. I can't. Andrea and I met at a time when we both knew what we wanted. We had lived our own separate lives before we became one. Our kind of love only happens to a very few people." Jason slowly took another sip of cognac.

Rudy looked at me and took my hand, saying, "I can feel your passion. I want no less for me. It will happen."

Struck by Rudy's intense energy, I knew then I was going with Rudy no matter what.

"The odds are against you. The impatience of youth, coupled with lack of worldly experience and self-identity will eventually set you apart."

"I'll beat the odds." Rudy said.

Sensing Dad's irritation, I quickly said, "Let's play pinball," As I escorted Rudy toward the game.

"Are you good at it?"

"Sometimes. Let me go first." Rudy agreed.

It didn't take long before my turn finished as I wanted to talk to Dad.

"Your turn. I'll be right back."

I walked over to Dad. He sat on a barstool, without an expression, staring at the train light going endlessly around and around.

"What do you think of him?" I cheerfully whispered, trying to break his somber mood.

Jason stared at his drink, pondering the question. "I can tell a lot about a person in a game of pool. It's a gentleman's sport, that's why I love it. I promised to be civilized. I've done that much. Sweet Basil, I'll always be here for you. First love is the hardest. I'll be patient with him."

Looking toward Rudy, Dad watched him for a second as he played pinball, "He is too self-assured. There's nothing wrong with that, except when it comes to love. I'm afraid his self-assurance will overshadow your confidence. First love usually clouds many things. Don't let him sweet talk you into things you don't want to do, okay? I'll tolerate him until the end. I love you too much not to."

You're the best, Daddy; he'll win you over. I know it."

Jason hugged me, said, "I've exceeded my civility for the night. I'll say good night."

He moved slowly from the barstool, turned to Rudy, saying, "Good night, Rudy. This evening has been no less than—stimulating."

Rudy smiled, saying, "Good night Dad. I'll be practicing for our next game. I'll be a worthy opponent."

"I've been playing for a long time; this isn't a game you master overnight."

"I'm the exception."

"Right." Jason left the room in a silent rage.

I sensed Dad's somberness, dismissed it thinking; Rudy won Maggie over he'll win Dad over too.

I went back to the pinball, watched Rudy play for hours. He was winning.

TWENTY-FIVE
Lives Change

Saturday morning could not come quick enough. I woke up feeling sensational—ready for my new life with Rudy. I quickly dressed, then continued packing.

Jason knocked on the closed bedroom door and then peeked in.

"Good morning. I did not believe you were leaving until now; this is the second darkest day of my life, the first your mother's death."

He reached into his pocket, handed me the car keys.

"Take the car. This way, you won't have an excuse to visit or leave when you want. Remember, don't take any disrespect. You are not obligated to stay."

"Things will be okay. You'll see Dad. Please don't worry. I'll come to visit after I get settled."

The phone rang. The emptiness of the room caused the rings to echo unusually loud. I grabbed the phone with celerity, as I felt Dad's somberness.

"Hello."

"Ready to crash a party?"

"Maggie. Where have you been?"

Trying to relieve the tension, Jason said, "Maggie, this will be a three-hour call. See you downstairs." Blowing a kiss toward me, he softly said, "Love you." Closing the door behind him.

The sound of Maggie's voice brought me instant joy.

118

"I called several times. We didn't connect," Maggie said.

"I have something to tell you. You're not going to believe this. I'm moving in with Rudy; Isn't that great? I started packing last night. A few more things, and done packing. I've been delirious for days!"

There was silence on the line; I could not even hear her breathe. "Hello, Maggie? Hello."

"I'm in shock. I can't believe you're doing this. I guess his mom liked you." Maggie said sarcastically.

"I thought you liked him."

"He's going too fast. What about school? Your career? Our traveling together?"

"Not a problem. I'm still doing all that, except Rudy will be there to help and support me. Everything is coming together quickly, but it's flawless. As Rudy said, 'You've got to take life by the balls,' and that's what I'm doing."

Maggie raised her voice, saying, "You're quoting him. It's too late. He has you. There is no turning back."

"Don't be absurd. We're friends. Forever, remember? I'm sure you'll meet someone soon. That doesn't mean our friendship is over, and it'll be more fun. We are starting to live. We're not high school kids anymore. We are on the verge of using our own ID cards."

"I know, I know. In my heart, we'll be friends forever, but things will not be the same. Our high school dreams are that, dreams. What does your dad think of this?"

"He's coming around. When he gets to know Rudy, he'll like him too. Now get a load of this; You're not going to believe it—I'm going to be living in the Heurtley House, it's magnificent. We can only use certain rooms, still, the Heurtley House. You'll have to come to see it for yourself. Say, you'll come by?"

Only half-listening, Maggie became upset. She said, "This makes up my mind."

"For what?"

"I'm joining the Air Force."

"Air Force? When did this start?"

"Seriously, about a month ago. It was going to be a surprise. This has been rolling in my brain since you made up your mind to be a flight attendant. You've talked about it for so long; I didn't think you would do it. So part of our dreams will come true."

Maggie paused for a moment to collect her thoughts and calm herself, then, she continued, "I hope you're not going to get mushy? Even worse, serious, you know I hate to get serious. It'll be fun. I'll get to see the world too. Maybe we can meet in an exotic country when you get your wings. I'll have rank by then. And maybe we can crash a party in a far off country. Wouldn't that be a riot, the stories we could tell at our ten-year school reunion? Getting busted and stuff."

"You'll do great, I know, but who's going to explain things to me? Who'll listen at four in the morning?" I said in a quivering voice.

Maggie whispered, "Rudy."

"It won't be the same. You know me as a sister. When do you make it official?"

"I already have. I leave in two weeks."

"Two weeks! You're leaving in two weeks?"

"Yes, sir, I told you it was a surprise. I tried calling a week ago to let you know it became official, and I guess you were with Rudy. That's okay. We have tons of memories, time for us to start making new ones."

"May I take you to the airport? Or wherever you have to go?"

"I'd rather you didn't. You're so emotional. I'll see ya when I see ya, okay?"

I couldn't hold back the tears, "Sure. See ya when I see ya."

"Bye," Maggie said.

Replacing the phone on its cradle, I kept my hand on it, imagined I held Maggie's hand. I talked to it, "We had so many plans, endless high school plans. Now I've found Rudy, and those plans are juvenile. Our adult lives have started. You'll have your adventures, and I'll have mine. We'll see each other again. It's only our beginning. Yeah, we'll have lots to talk about in a few months. Bye, Maggie."

I felt lonely saying good-bye to Maggie, yet excited I'd soon be with Rudy. I finished packing. I couldn't handle any more sadness.

Dad heard me come downstairs asked, "Need help? What's wrong? Why are you crying?"

"It's okay, Dad; I only have these suitcases and a shoulder bag." Sniffling, I continued, "Maggie told me she joined the Air Force. I can't believe it. She's leaving in two weeks."

"She's in for quite an adventure. She'll be fine. Maggie can take care of herself."

"Yeah, I know. It made me sad cause I didn't know about it. We tell each other everything. Always. Things are happening too fast. We can't keep up."

"Change your mind? You can stay."

"No, Dad, let's say good-bye for now, okay."

Hugging, we were teary-eyed.

Walking through the doorway, I took a deep breath said, "It'll be all right. You'll see."

"Take care, Sweet Basil. See you soon."

Dad watched in disbelief, like the final punch of a boxing match, watching the favorite go down.

Jason waved until I was no longer in sight.

Driving toward Oak Park, joy and excitement dissipated my sadness about Maggie and about leaving home. I'd soon be with Rudy.

TWENTY-SIX
Lust

Waiting by the driveway, Rudy smiled; his demeanor instantly put me in a state of giddiness. This moment had to be a beautiful dream, and I could only share these fantasies with him. His voice confirmed my being.

He opened the car door, "I was counting the minutes of your arrival." Helping me step out into his arms, he hugged and kissed me.

"Let's go inside."

"What about my things?"

"We'll get them later."

We slowly walked toward the house hand in hand. I could feel his explosive energy. His jet black hair sparkled in the twilight. His lips, perfectly shaped, brought memories of his kisses.

Rudy softly said at the entrance, "I want to carry you over the threshold, my precious."

I smiled, feeling stupendous.

"Okay." The only word I could utter.

He tenderly picked me up. His embrace, a blanket of strength and security, carried me over and beyond into my fantasy world. When he put me down, we were in the fabulous living room.

Rudy had lit five white candles, and incense burned, drifting an exquisite aroma into the room. He had poured white wine in a pair of golden goblets.

122

"What is that arousing scent?"

"It's a mixture of herbs and oils. Ms. Julia makes it. I've never asked what's in it. I don't want to know. This way, it's mysteriously erotic."

We sat on the floor on top of a fluffy white comforter surrounded by white candles. It gave the illusion of being in a warm cave. Engulfed by natures burning hidden desires, Rudy came closer. He gently pressed his luscious lips to my lips—his tongue intertwined with mine—the kiss, mystical and vibrant. Before I knew it, we were lying on the floor. The excitement in the air felt rapturous. So pleasing and undeniable, Rudy continued his kisses. I had not realized he had opened my blouse.

"Rudy. I've never done this before. I'm a virgin."

Rudy's mesmerizing licorice black eyes gazed into mine.

"We'll go slow. Don't be frightened. Relax. Enjoy my body. Together this will be the best copulation on the planet."

With that, I gave myself to him. He was in control, and I followed his direction. His engorged manhood was more than I could handle. Rudy stopped to open a condom.

"We'll put this on together."

He directed my hands with provocative skill.

"Unroll it gently precious, take as long as you want."

The unrolling became fabulous—the fit, stunning.

"You're so gifted. That was sensational." Rudy remarked.

I smiled at him innocently.

"I love that look."

He kissed my entire body, giving me uncontrollable excitement. We rolled on the comforter as one, my expectations at that moment fulfilled beyond my dreams and fantasies. The rhapsody and elation I felt were voracious. I would be his forever. When we stopped, we were breathless.

"Are you all right?" Rudy asked.

I looked at him, lovingly whispered, "The best copulation on the planet."

We laughed. Laying side by side, we were in complete tranquillity and unity.

"Let's drink some wine, get dressed, and bring in your things."

As his lips envelop mine anew, I fulminated with desire. Hoping this would never end.

Rudy whispered, "I wanted you, needed you. I didn't have the willpower anymore."

He kissed me again and again, finally saying, "Forget your things, for now, let's continue in the bedroom."

Fervently I agreed.

Rudy picked me up, kissed me gently, and carried me to the bedroom.

The only decoration in the bedroom was the Ankh, perfectly centered on the wall above the bed.

"So what's the other meaning of the Egyptian cross?"

Rudy delicately put me on the bed, tenderly kissed my neck, saying, "The staff indicates the male. The closed-loop indicates the female." He tenderly eased up to my moist lips, said, "Together, it means the union of the male and female."

We kissed seductively, erotically, inducing the pure lustful passion overflowing within me, our explosive union, mystical. Unforgettable.

Breathless, Rudy said, "You'll be mine always."

TWENTY-SEVEN
Lust or Love

Sage said softly, "That's it, Mother. Now, do you understand? If I can't go back to Rudy, I won't go back."

Carefully Andrea said, "Sweet Basil, you are confusing lust for love. Dad gave good advice; young men desire sex and lust except, young women do too. Sex and lust are not a one gender emotion. Initially, everyone is overwhelmed by the body's desires. Natural urges, once experienced, lust will turn to love, most of the time. The chaste era is over. That's all—another stage of growth. Sadly, I think you weren't alive long enough. You haven't outgrown the lustful stage. I haven't gotten over your innocent stage. I see you as my five-year-old, the innocence of life, a time of true unconditional love. As youth ages and innocence fades, unconditional love must become conditional, or it becomes deadly love. Conditional love allows adults to understand new adults, to guide them onto the right path of life. The patience conditional love requires transforms new adults into adults, continuing the passage to the next generation.

Had you lived beyond the lust, you would understand. You would see Rudy for what he was, an egotistical womanizer. He used you for his pleasures. He knew you were a naïve girl, a virgin. After he tired of you, he left. That's the kind of man he is. He may change, but it's doubtful. Young womanizers become old womanizers, always users."

Teary-eyed, Andrea lovingly looked at her daughter, touched her pale, delicate face, then continued, "I want you to know unconditional love as I did.

You won't find it with Rudy."

Sage cried, "Mother, let me go back to Rudy or the oblivion crypt. I don't want existence if I can't have Rudy. I don't want to live without his touch, his essence." Pausing, Sage looked at her mother, murmured, "That's it. I don't want to talk anymore. Let me go."

Maintaining her composure, Andrea said, "We've come this far. I'll agree to send you back to Rudy. Albeit deep in my heart, I know it is not okay."

"Thank you. Thank you. Thank you, mother. It'll be phenomenal." Sage hugged her mother joyfully.

Devoted to her daughter, Andrea explained, "I can only send you back as a baby. That's one of the only rules to going back. An adult was allowed to go back thousands of years ago, treachery and disaster occurred. Adults are forbidden to go back. An innocent baby will not forsake."

Sage's eyes gleamed with joy.

"You'll be in a state of deep sleep. Sleeping in the catacomb until the time is right for your rebirth."

Andrea waved her hand and breathed gently over Sage.

"This will keep your physical body intact, allowing the soul to remain calm." Putting Sage in deep repose, Andrea's final words were, "Remember me always."

Clayton became mortified, angered at recalling the events. He had to maintain composure, the fear of upsetting the baby haunted him.

"Why didn't she stop? Andrea was confused, and that confusion brought their demise. Oh little angel, the shame of it all. When will the human soul learn? We should never attempt at playing God! That has been the downfall of mankind since the beginning of time. Alas, the shame of it all."

Needing to find his peace, Clayton hugged the baby, sang the fourth soothing verse to Amazing Grace.

He continued reminiscing of the events Andrea had told him. Events that brought demise to his beloved family, would he succumb to the same?

Part Three
The Rebirth
"It's a girl?"

TWENTY-EIGHT
Rudy and Sarah

The distractions in the sterile room were the bright lights and a few distinctive sound noises, Sarah being the focus of attention. Her dark brown hair was wet with perspiration. Her big brown eyes, usually surrounded by make-up, were unadorned and tired—a voice encouraging her to breathe methodically.

"Remember the Lamaze method."

"They didn't tell me it would be twelve hours of excruciating pain," Sarah screamed.

The calm voice continued, "We can see the head now. Any minute it'll be over. Continue breathing. Breathe. Push. Here are the shoulders. Beautiful. We did it!"

Exhausted, Sarah cried out, "Boy or girl? Is it healthy?"

Trying to catch her breath asked, "Healthy? Is it healthy?" Her patience had long been exhausted.

"It's a girl. She's beautiful and healthy." Rudy said, kissing Sarah tenderly on the forehead.

"Have you selected a name?" The doctor asked.

"Yes. Sage. Her name is Sage." Rudy said immediately.

The experienced doctor tied and severed the umbilical cord. Holding the trophy in his safe hands, he brought the baby girl to the tired mother saying, "Welcome to the world, Sage. Meet your Mom."

The equally experienced obstetric nurse took the baby for clean-up, weighing, and vital signs saying, "You were fantastic, Sarah. We'll take you back to your room; we will bring your baby shortly."

Back in the room, Sarah quietly asked Rudy, "Where did Sage enter into our choice of names? What happened to Mary Rose? I thought we agreed, Mary Rose for a girl or Rory Allen for a boy."

"It's a name reminding me of beauty. Good times. Seeing the baby reminded me of the name Sage," Rudy said nonchalantly.

Before Sarah could ask any more questions, the door opened. The same obstetric nurse brought in the baby.

Sounding apologetic, the nurse said, "I normally don't bring the babies to the parents—a nursing assistant does; however, I had to tell you two this is the most beautiful baby I've ever seen. Her skin has already cleared up. She has lustrous ebony hair."

The nurse changed her tone, sounded more like a nurse training her student nurses. "Newborns have greyish blue eyes and eventually change to their true color. Her eyes are different. She has a glimpse of green in her eyes." The nurse's enthusiasm returned in her voice, saying, "Sage is going to have beautiful, green eyes. I've been in obstetrics for a long time. I have never seen such a perfect baby. She looks like a porcelain doll. I hope she brings you much joy and happiness." She handed the baby to Sarah.

Looking at her baby, Sarah smiled in contentment, emphatically said, "She is beautiful." Sarah gently caressed the tiny cheek.

Standing beside her, Rudy vehemently agreed. "She is precious."

Sarah did not give the name change a second thought. Proud of their miracle, all the labor pains, all discussions, were forgotten.

Sarah exclaimed, "Our Sage will be loved, unconditionally."

TWENTY-NINE
Birthday Party

Sarah looked out the kitchen window, watching the kids frolicking and teasing each other. "Eleven. Hard to believe Sage is eleven. Her first birthday party where she wanted to invite boys tickled me so much; I had to write an entry in the journal."

"How can you be tickled? Boys are in her life now. Soon, she'll abandon us, doesn't make me happy. I want to show her everything about life. Not some boy." Rudy remarked, annoyed.

"Rudy, it's only a little kid's party, not her wedding. Get over it. Let's get ready to take them to the zoo."

Sarah stepped outside, called the children together.

Rudy continued looking out the window as the cold water from the faucet filled a glass. Seeing his gorgeous daughter strolling along with the other children, he drank from the glass as he continued his obsessive thought, "I'll show you everything, not some boy."

In a commanding motherly fashion, Sarah shouted, "Six of you come with me in the van. Five go in the car with Rudy."

The giggles of little girls and roguishness of little boys encircled Sarah. Little voices bellowing, "I don't want to sit by Nathan. I won't sit by Ralph. I want a window. I have to go to the bathroom."

Still in control, she shouted to be heard. Sarah said, "Okay, kids. The boys go with Rudy, the girls with me. And whoever has to go to the

130

bathroom go now."

The girls hollered, "Ye-e-eah!"

The girls ran and skipped toward the van, settling in. The boys ran toward the car, jumped in, trying to settle in, turning toward the van, the boys made faces at the girls.

Thirty minutes later, they arrived at Brookfield Zoo. As Sarah paid for everyone, Nathan made faces and animal noises at people passing.

Once on the zoo grounds, Sarah instructed, "Everyone, listen. If you want, you're on your own, or you can come with Rudy and me. If you go on your own, make sure to meet back here. In front of this building at two o'clock. We will go in together to see the seal show."

The girls went off together. The boys followed closely behind.

"You want ice cream? Gotta have an ice cream cone at the zoo," Sarah asked Rudy.

Rudy watched the kids leave, his attention entirely on Sage.

"How could you let them go by themselves?"

Starting to get irritable, Sarah vented, "They'll be fine. They don't want to be with grown-ups. Let them enjoy their childhood. It'll be gone before they know it. Lighten up."

Sarah didn't wait for Rudy to respond. She grabbed his arm, "The ice cream shop is this way," She escorted him in the opposite direction.

Arriving home, the kids stepped out of the vehicles tired. Some of the kids grabbed their zoo treasures. Sage and several of the girls bought helium-filled balloons. Tilly and Cindy each bought a stuffed seal. Ralph laughed and poked at any balloon he could reach. Portly, Nathan grabbed his bag of peanuts, which were supposed to feed the elephants. He also held a pair of large framed sunglasses he put on. Everybody laughed at seeing the little boy with the colossal glasses, including Nathan, the clown of the group.

Sarah beamed with delight, as it had been a terrific day, telling the children, "Thanks for not getting lost. You were all perfect, and we hope everyone had a wonderful time. Good night."

Tired voices responded, "Good night."

The kids ran off toward their waiting parents except for Ralph, who lived next door. He scampered home. Rudy and Sarah waved at the parents and waited for Ralph to go inside his house. Joyfully, Sage ran toward their house.
Rudy and Sarah followed closely behind.

"This is the best birthday party I've ever had," Sage hugged her mom and dad, then scurried to her room.

The evening went quick. Everyone sat at the dinner table, exhausted.

Sage softly said, "Mom, I'm not hungry. My stomach hurts."

Understandably, Sarah said, "We ate lots of junk food, and it's been a long day Sweetie. We'll be up to tuck in."

"Thanks, Mom."

Leaving her dinner untouched, the tired little girl trudged up to her bedroom.

Rudy and Sarah peeked into Sage's room. She slept soundly. The light from the full moon seeped into the bedroom, casting an angelic glow around her.

"My gifted daughter is safe," Rudy whispered.

Sarah quietly agreed, "This was a great day. She and her friends had a fantastic time. I have to write about this entire day in her journal. Boys."

Sarah giggled as she made her way toward their bedroom. Her thoughts of writing every memory for her little girl jumbled in her head. The crazy gibberish would make sense in the journal.

Rudy closed the door, leaving their little girl sleeping peacefully in her dreams.

Part Four
Deadly Love
"What's wrong?"

THIRTY
The Hospital

The silence of the night awakened by piercing screams coming from Sage's room.

Sarah jumped out of bed, followed by Rudy.

Entering the moonlit room, depicted a grey figure on the bed. Turning on the light, they saw Sage wrenched in pain.

"What's wrong?" Sarah shouted.

"I-I hurt. My stomach."

"This isn't a normal stomachache. Maybe she got food poisoning at the zoo. Let's take her to the emergency room."

Running back to their bedroom, Sarah slipped on a jogging suit, screaming, "Hurry, Rudy, hurry."

Following Sarah, Rudy slipped on jeans and a tee-shirt.

"Go get the car. I'll wrap her up and bring her out." Rudy followed the orders without question.

Like a madwoman, Sarah grabbed a blanket from the hall closet, ran back to Sage's room.

Sage was holding her stomach. Her little body was shaking and her hair drenched in sweat. Sarah gently wiped her little girl's brow, wrapped her as if she were an infant. As she wrapped her daughter, she noticed a small amount of blood on the bed.

"This is not a normal stomachache. Hold on, baby. Mommy will protect you." Lifting her baby, she went out the door, whisper shouting, "Hurry,

Rudy, hurry!"

The screeching tires stopped the car in front of the emergency room. Holding her daughter, Sarah effortlessly flew out of the car into the hospital. Nurses quickly surrounded them. Someone brought a Gurney. Sarah gently put her baby on the stretcher.

A clinical voice asked, "What's the problem?"

Unnerved, Sarah explained, "She keeps saying her stomach hurts. It looks like she has some sort of bleeding too. I don't understand that; I don't understand the bleeding. Please make it stop. Hurry, make it stop."

"Calm down, Ma'am. A doctor will be right with her. In the meantime, come with me. You need to fill out some insurance papers and some release forms. What's your name?" The nurse asked cordially.

"Sarah."

Someone wheeled Sage into an exam room.

Sobbing, Sarah watched as the door closed. The nurse chaperons Sarah to the check-in desk.

Sarah, waiting in the lobby, sees Rudy.

"Where have you been?" She immediately seethed.

"I've been looking for parking—every space in the immediate area reserved for doctors or employees. I found a spot on the sixth level, and the elevators are out of order. I ran down four flights of stairs. Ultimately, on the second level, the elevators were working. I took one to the ER, but I was in the wrong wing. I've been frantic; what's happening to Sage?"

"Why didn't you park in the damn towing zone?" Exhausted, Sarah realized what she had said.

"I'm sorry," She hugged Rudy, said, "I don't know anything yet. She's still in the exam room."

Rudy and Sarah sat on the lobby couch holding hands in silence.

Physically and emotionally depleted, Sarah's head dropped on Rudy's shoulder as she fell asleep.

"Rudy, Sarah?"

Rudy softly shook Sarah awake.

A haggard man in hospital scrubs approached them, "Hi. I'm Doctor Bennett."

"How's my daughter? What's wrong with her? When can I see her?" Sarah asked.

"I'd rather we talked in a more private environment. Come this way to my office."

"Lead the way," Sarah said, seizing her purse.

They followed the Doctor to a cluttered office. Files stacked everywhere, including the floor.

The doctor made his way through a pathway, walking carefully to a messy desk.

He asked them to sit. Two well worn reddish-brown leather chairs were in front of the desk.

"Sorry about this place. We're very short-handed, this doesn't mean the staff isn't professional. We have a top-notch crew." The doctor said. He looked tired, far away, and analytically continued, "This has been a strange night. Full moons are like that; I don't have statistics to prove it, though. It's just my observation. Some day I'm going to write a paper on the effects of the full moon on the human psyche. Animals and plants are affected too." He appeared to be in his world, oblivious to the present.

Delirious, Sarah shouted, "Doctor, please. What's happened to my daughter?"

Looking at Rudy and Sarah, without emotion, the Doctor stated, "I don't know how to say this as there are no right words. Your daughter had a spontaneous abortion."

"That's impossible. My baby hasn't even started her period. It's a mistake. Have you checked for food poisoning? We ate at the zoo. It's food poisoning. Tell him, Rudy," Sarah shrieked in horror.

Emotionless, Doctor Bennett continued, "Sarah, try to compose yourself. There was fetal tissue. She has lost an excessive amount of blood. Your daughter is in critical condition."

Sounding analytical again, he continued, "Premenstrual pregnancies are very rare, exceedingly rare. Historically, the ones medically diagnosed usually terminate. The scenario could be, your daughter was having

136

intercourse before her menses. She started with sperm being present."

The fatigued Doctor finally noticed Sarah's horror. He concluded, "Well, you know the rest."

Sarah screamed, "I want to see her now."

Weary, Doctor Bennett stood, went around the desk. He placed his hands on Sarah's shoulders and further explained, "Because of her age, I have to report this to social services. There will be an investigation and lots of questions. Please try to calm yourself. The next few days will be offensive, ghastly, and grueling for you."

Looking at Sarah with a little compassion now, he patted her on the shoulder, "I'll take you to her."

Feebly, Sarah followed the Doctor with Rudy silent at her side.

THIRTY-ONE
Secrets

Sarah's eyes were red and puffed from lack of sleep, more so from crying. She sat staring at her daughter. Rudy walked in meekly.

"Sarah, you have to eat something. Let's go home and freshen up."

Almost as lifeless as her daughter, Sarah mumbled, "No."

"You can't stay like this. You have to start being rational."

"I will not leave her," Sarah growled.

She tenderly stroked her daughter's petite arm and then her lusterless hair.

"I'll go home. Bring you some clean clothes." Looking down, softly finished saying, "and something to eat."

Sarah stared at her little girl as Rudy left the room.

Hours passed.

A sound finally emitted from the silent bed and at once aroused Sarah. Automatically she reached for the tiny hand and whispered, "Sage. I'm here. Mommy is here."

Languid Sage quietly spoke, "I'm thirsty."

Sarah quickly poured water from the bed stand pitcher, gently bringing the glass to Sage's lips. She did not have the strength to drink.

Sarah wet her fingers delicately smoothed the dry miniature lips with cool water.

Brave-hearted Sarah whispered, "Who did this to you, baby?" Her eyes, fueled with tears, tried to maintain control.

"Who hurt you?"

The timid, frail little voice uttered, "Daddy told me not to tell anyone. Ever. They would take him away if I told."

Sarah became enraged as she heard her little girl's words. Her will sucked out of her body.

"You can tell Mommy anything, Sweetie," Sarah said as calmly as she could, trying to comfort her child.

Sage's voice dwindled. No more words.

Sarah felt hate. Hated Rudy, hated herself. Life itself.

She reached back for the chair, sat in a zombie-like state. Tears overflowed down her face uncontrollably, were the only clues to her being alive.

Sarah had lost the concept of time; it didn't matter as long as her baby was in this condition. She would not move until she saw her little girl smile again.

A groaning sound beckoned. Sarah immediately stood by the bed.

A squeamish voice said, "Mommy. I saw a beautiful lady. She said her name is Andrea, and you have to say good-bye."

"Baby, don't listen to her. Listen to me. I'll take care of you now. We have so much to do, your cotillion, first boyfriend, the prom, graduation. Your first car. Come back to me. We'll do those things and more. Baby, please get better."

"I can't. I hurt again; I hurt too much. I," The little girl's voice faded.

Her beautiful, enthralling green eyes were lifeless. Slowly her eyes became slits, then nothing, eyelids that didn't move.

Frantically Sarah reached for the call button. The monitors attached to Sage, erratic. Sarah glared at them, not knowing what it meant. She looked down at her daughter, the little eyes shut. Sarah tried opening the eyelids. She saw nothing but white eyeballs. Sage's little body became still.

"Come back so I can stop the hurt," Sarah screamed.

A nurse entered the room and, without hesitation, calmly called, "Doctor

Blue in the ICU. Repeat. Doctor Blue in the ICU."

The nurse rushed to the monitor and told Sarah to wait in the lobby. Promptly the small area filled with medical personnel. Doctor Bennet approached rapidly.

"Please help her, Doctor Bennett," Sarah pleaded.

Stopping for a moment, the doctor snapped, "Please wait in the lobby so we can do our job. We will call you if we need you."

Dazed, Sarah obeyed and ambled to the lobby.

Rudy walked into the hospital lobby, carrying Sarah's clothes under his left arm and holding a cola. His right hand with a tray of burgers and fries, he spotted her walking up and down the corridor.

Sarah also saw him. Deranged, she ran toward him. She pounded his chest, kicked his groin, and screamed, "You bastard. I hate you. You son of a bitch."

Rudy dropped everything, trying to protect himself. Most of the cola splashed him, and the corrugated food tray slid on the shiny linoleum floor. Sarah grasped the clothes, ripping them; she had lost control.

A security guard saw the commotion. He ran to the scene, apprehended Sarah. "Lady. Calm down. Please calm down," He urged.

Some people stared, others carefully avoiding the spilled food, little kids pointed as if they knew what had happened.

The security guard now firmly held Sarah's once maniacal arms. At last, she became docile. The guard loosened his grip. Sarah put her face in her hands, crying irrepressibly. Another guard came to assist.

"Help me escort them to the security office and get a cleaning crew over here. Now," The flushed guard ordered.

Sitting quiescent in the security office, Sarah glared at Rudy.

"How could you violate our daughter? You're supposed to protect her, not hurt her. You're her guardian. That means to guard, you shithead. You monster. You're worse than the devil. At least the devil has a purpose. You have no reason for this malicious, hideous act."

For the first time, tears were in Rudy's eyes, "I did have a reason," He said softly.

Horrified, Sarah rumbled, "You're justifying this rape!"

Detached, Rudy slowly stood and spewed out, "I thought I could handle it. Remember, when she was born, I told you the name reminded me of beauty and good times. Sage was the name of my only true love. She died years ago. And adored me; she would do anything for me. As our Sage started growing up, I began seeing her as my Sage, my true love. I had to have her again. I wasn't violating our daughter. I lusted and loved my Sage. I had to,"

Sarah clenched her fist, viciously hit Rudy on the side of his head. The shock made him stagger.

"Shut up, you bastard. Shut up, you turd!"

The entire time scratched and hit Rudy anywhere she could. She pulled his hair; a clump ended up in her clenched fist. She threw it at him, tried to grab another chunk of hair.

The security guard rushed over, stood between them, trying to control Sarah.

"Keep him away from me. You fuckin' bastard. You named my daughter after an old girlfriend—demented freak. When I leave here, I'm changing her name. I will see to it you rot in jail. I'm pressing charges. You'll never forget this as long as I'm alive."

Fuming at the guard, she commanded, "Call the police. This piece of shit is a child molester. I can't stand being in the same room with him."

The security guard instructed Rudy to go to another desk across the room. Rudy slowly shuffled to the desk as Sarah took one last swat.

Breathing heavy, trying to gain control, Sarah vehemently pleaded, "Please let me go. My baby is in intensive care. I don't know if she is alive or dead. Please." Sympathetic, the guard remarked, "You'll have to come back to fill out papers."

"Undeniably. I won't let this bastard get away," She shouted as she ran out the door.

Hurriedly finding her way back to the ICU, the corridor seemed empty, too silent. She approached her little girl's room, and the empty feeling grew deeper. The silence became eerie. Sarah's body seemed to be in slow motion. Entering the room, a part of her died at sight.

"No-o-o-o-o!"

The white sheet neatly tucked under Sage's pale chin became an overwhelming sight. Her baby lay lifeless. A nurse entered the room, attempted to comfort her, the comfort was inutile.

Emotionless, Sarah said, "I was supposed to protect her. How could I let this happen? Why was I blinded? I never suspected a thing; my little girl never
complained. How can there be a God to allow this horrible thing to happen? I hope there is a hell; certainly, Rudy will be there. I will follow him, killing him over and over, for the rest of eternity, our perpetual misery. Deserving nothing less for what my beautiful little girl endured. Unknowingly, we lived in evil, with the devil himself."

Siphoned of tears, Sarah managed a faint smile whispered, "Hopefully, you're in a celestial paradise, baby. Forgive me." She bent over the lifeless, cold body, kissed her little girl one last time.

"Good-bye, Mary Rose. I love you."

The nurse compassionately guided Sarah out of the room.

Part Five
True Death
"Deadly love."

THIRTY-TWO
Andrea's Shrills

The formless entity softly echoed, "Sage. Come back to me. Remember me always."

A touch without hands soothed Sage's form. The voice continued the soothing chant, "Remember me always."

Andrea needed all the energy she could generate. The personification required too much vital energy. Only her essence, her soul, would maintain them now. She alone possessed the desire for this solace encounter.

A silent shift, a faint voice arose from Sage's disappearing physical body, "Who are you? Are you the lady I've been hearing? I can't see. Why can't I see?"

The sound of the frail little girl made Andrea's soul melancholy; however, her voice had brilliance.

"Yes. I'm Andrea. I wanted your pain to stop. Please don't say too much. The more energy you use, the quicker the end will come. I want our brief encounter to last as long as possible. You can't see me because you don't have the energy. You're too fragile to view my soul. I can't help you. Soon we'll go separate ways. Before we leave, I want you to listen. I need your forgiveness. We met before—I was your first mother."

Andrea choked on hearing her own words; she tried wholeheartedly to remember tranquillity. Her voice trembled. She had to maintain calmness.

"My love for you is unconditional. I wanted you to have another chance at life. For you to know love as I did. We talked. Blinded by my love, I became convinced to send you back to Rudy. Knowing there is bountiful love in the physical world. I put my fears aside. My conjecture was wrong. Your unconditional love for Rudy was wrong. I failed to accept the evilness hidden in Rudy. His fetish for you became purely self-gratifying. He had a choice, stop the lust for a daughter or act upon it. He chose to gratify himself."

Andrea had to pause, her voice becoming shaky, her aura had shades of grey, anger seeping in. Regaining her temperament, she slowly continued, "Your feelings were so innocent, yet your instinct not developed. I followed those trusting instincts and made a terrible mistake. We should have crossed into the spirit world but, I could not see beyond my desires. They became obsessive, and I sanctioned it by good thoughts. How can good wishes go bad?

Andrea's soul floated in silence, realizing the truth.

"Ar-r-r-gh!" Screams from Andrea's soul were drilling. "I stayed in the physical body too long. I became obsessed."

Andrea's realization became maddening. Her cries echoed in the catacomb. Her soul's energy engulfed Sage's form, trying to attain solace and peace. She could not find it.

Sage's small form not cognizant, fading. Andrea had to maintain control to continue, slightly longer. She had to support both energies. Thinking of her utopia, she managed to take hold of the energy needed. Both entities glowed again.

"I unknowingly acquired corrupt emotions. I knew being in the physical form, I would not be immune to these vicious emotions. I disregarded the decadence of the physical world for my desires. I should have backed off, stopped at once, and crossed us over. I should have let the catacomb complete the transition."

Andrea's screams reverberated in the emptiness of the catacomb. The two virtually lifeless forms were one. The peace not there; Andrea struggled to hold on. This is going too fast. She fought within herself for more energy.

145

Suddenly, she realized the problem–she was fighting it.

She withdrew from Sage, leaving the dying form unprotected. Two entities again, she let her formless soul float. She needed to meditate on splendid
memories. The radiance of being in the spirit world soothed her, bringing peace and love.

Her glorious form once again a healing light, she surrounded the little form as if in a mother's womb, protecting Sage from hostile dominion.

"A little longer, this agony will end. Sweet Basil, I want you to know I put us on the edge of death because of my unconditional love for you. Upon meditation, I discovered something horrible. I sent you back for me. I was selfish. Of all the negative emotions, selfishness tops the list, ranked with hate. My unconditional love turned corrupt—it turned into deadly love. Please forgive me, Sweet Basil."

The formless little entity faintly gasped, "There is nothing to forgive. I did know unconditional love—your love. The way you said, Sweet Basil, coupled with your touch, brought back wonderful memories only unconditional love transcends. I have your unconditional love in me."

Hearing those words, Andrea solemnly said, "I can't change what I allowed to happen. Your soul must go to the oblivion crypt, the deadly sacrifice when things go wrong."

Andrea engulfed the little form. Feeling the peace and love she sought. Ironically great pain ensued. Knowing, their time had ended.

The tiny form within her started to disappear, slowly diminished from her once protective soul. The tremendous pain of losing her baby, knowing it was her fault, made her shriek unmercifully.

A doorway opened. Aunt Rita swiftly engulfed Andrea, taking her to the other side.

The shrill of Andrea's torment, along with Sage's soul, quietly vanished from the darkness of the catacomb into the depths of the oblivion crypt.

THIRTY-THREE
Jason

On May 6, 2016, the old man silently sat in a wheelchair. His soon to be new home, an eight by ten room. The room contained a single bed with a grey mattress—a nightstand with a small lamp placed in the middle. The lampshade belonged in an antique shop long ago. Dingy green floral curtains covered a window, where a little ray of sunshine tried to peek through. A perky voice broke up the stillness.

"Hi, Jason. I'm Hortensia. Call me Babs. Everybody does–they say I babble too much. I don't think so, and I'm just full of energy, love people, and my job. I'm your Aide. I'll make up your bed and inventory your belongings. I'll make sure everything is labeled. Sometimes laundry loses stuff. But if things are marked, they'll eventually get back to their owner."

The chubby young woman worked quickly to make the bed. Adding sheets and a blanket to the cold looking bed somehow gave it an inviting appearance. She opened the curtains. The evening sun-splashed into the room like a yellow paintbrush gone crazy; it brought cheeriness to the drab surroundings. Babs plopped the heavy suitcase on the bed.

"Is this the only suitcase you have? I didn't see any other belongings brought to your room. Most residents in a private room bring lots of things. If anything is missing, tell me, and I will hunt them down, no problem."

Tired from his trip, Jason only wanted to sleep. It had been a long time since he had flown anywhere. The airport excitement, waiting for porters and cabs had drained his old fatigued body.

"I learned a long time ago to travel light. Besides, I don't plan on staying long."

Babs continued to mark his clothes, reminiscent of youthful times preparing for summer camp.

"What do you mean not staying long? You've come a long way for Respite Care. Your chart indicates you moved here from Chicago. What brought you to Roswell?"

The questions brought a smile to Jason's tired face, "The aliens."

Babs laughed. Before she could say a word, Jason continued.

"Everybody is right. You sure like to babble. If you must know, I saw an advertisement in a magazine. The inviting, colorful ad read something like, 'Calling Winds Inn. Rooms for the chronologically enhanced. Personal care, twenty-four hours a day in private surroundings. No schedules, no routines. You are the boss. Call now.' So I did, and here I am."

"But why aren't you staying?"

"Because you are going to bore me to death with all your questions. I'm tired. I need sleep. I want to go to bed."

Babs' small dark eyes opened wide, promptly saying, "Oh, Jason. I'm sorry. Yes. Right away."

Her chubby body became nimble, and she quickly finished marking the clothes. She found a small brass double picture frame at the bottom of the clothes. She took the photos, placed them carefully on the nightstand. Taking the empty suitcase, she put it neatly in the closet. She rushed and came back to the bed, brought the covers down, and fluffed the pillow again.

"Do you need help going to the bathroom? Something to drink? Please, Jason, whatever you need."

"No, I need to sleep now. Help me out of this contraption and into bed." Jason banged on the wheelchair armrest as he tried to get up.

Babs graciously went by his side. Assisted him with his clothes, helped him to bed. Mothering over Jason, tucked the sheets. Lastly, she made sure the pitcher had fresh ice water.

"Anything else?" Not waiting for him to answer, she pointed to the bedrail instructing him.

"This is your call light; if you need anything, press here. And I'll be here as soon as possible."

Jason chuckled, said, "I think I'd rather call the space aliens."

Babs laughed too.

"You're all right, Jason. We're going to get along just fine. Good night," She quietly left the room.

Jason slowly rolled over. His crooked boney fingers raised the covers over his head, bringing him to a peaceful sleep.

Aroused by the morning sunlight, Jason moved sluggishly. The oversized illuminated wall clock displayed 6:30. He yawned, slowly got up, and shuffled to the bathroom. He relieved himself, then slowly shuffled back toward the window. His hazy aged eyes looked outside. He could not believe the beautiful sunrise. Morning grey clouds, highlighted by vibrant red-orange sun rays, on a magnificent canvass of Mediterranean blue sky—hypnotic, he thought. I haven't seen something this beautiful since Andrea, a pleasant way to leave this earthly existence, watching the simplistic beauty only nature can produce.

A knock at the door interrupted his thoughts.

"Good morning Jason. Ready for some breakfast? I brought you a menu," Babs entered cheerfully.

Jason turned, inched his way toward the wheelchair. His old legs depleted quickly of strength.

"Good morning Babs. I'm sorry I was short-tempered yesterday."

Babs ran over to him, helped him sit on the chair.

"Don't give it a second thought. You were right. I tend to run off at the mouth at times."

"At times? Babs."

Both laughed.

"I have coffee, orange, grapefruit, or tomato juices. Oh, prune juice too. I'll place your breakfast order, and you'll be eating in no time."

"Coffee and tomato juice. The only breakfast I want is toast."

"I've got toast in my food cart. Do you want jam?"

She didn't wait for Jason to answer as she hastily walked to the doorway and opened the food cart. She took a tray, put two toast and a mini-pot of coffee on it. Placing a snack table in front of Jason, she then placed the food tray on it.

"Hold on." She said without further explanation.

She ran to the other side of the cart, where she grabbed a tomato juice and grape jam. Walked back, she smiled, setting that on the tray too.

"Now, be careful with the coffee. It's scorching. Here, let me pour the first cup. Anything else?"

Without hesitation, Jason slowly said, "Thank you, Babs. This is excellent. I'll work on this while watching the marvelous sunrise."

Babs departed, leaving Jason in far off thoughts.

Jason looked at the faded, cracked pictures; his memories could not imagine them old.

He slowly chewed the toast. Begged in silence, I'm ready to be with you. This blissful place has brought memories of happy times long gone.

I am ready to be with you.

THIRTY-FOUR
Clayton

Clayton slowly exhaled, said, "This is where I became involved, Little angel, this is first-hand knowledge of what happened next. He looked at the innocent angel, cautiously continued.

"Alma and I ponder on who would be the third energy to form Jason's trinity. We were happy he would soon join us. We couldn't wait for him to let go of his physical body. It's a thrill to wait for a loved one every time. The anticipation is always exhilarating. It makes the waiting souls stronger. Those involved in the trinity are illuminated souls waiting for the transition and the new soul's eventual cross over. His mother and I were discussing either one of his grandmothers. He would like that. Even though Jason never met my mother. But things changed drastically as somehow Andrea's energy permeated our space."

Andrea humbly asked, "Alma. Clayton. I beseech you to allow me to be a part of Jason's trinity. Also, may I be the guide? Please relinquish your guiding rights to me. I beg you, let me be Jason's guide."

She indeed asked a lot; selected guides are not random choices. The chosen guides are parents and blood relatives. It is a beautiful, exhilarating event. To relinquish it to a spouse or friend is possible, though it doesn't happen often.

I also knew about Sage's death. The death of any soul brings much sadness. Death causes the rippling of souls, like sound waves on water. A heavenly minute of repose for any soul's death is required, allowing peace and the ripple to stop.

I asked Andrea point-blank, "What are your intentions? We know Jason loved you very much. We are certain he would be pleased to see you. We also know about the demise of our granddaughter. Jason will be devastated. What are your intentions?"

Andrea said, "I must be the one to tell Jason what happened to Sage. Please let me guide him."

Feeling her pain, Alma and I consented to the transfer.

I said, "Be Jason's guide. You two were meant to be together, eternally"

Andrea glowed at the response.

"We trusted Andrea. Being in paradise doesn't make you psychic, little angel. It does make you trustworthy of all who are here. Trust and love are all I've known since I've been here. The Almighty Spirit is the only entity that knows someone's true feelings. However, the Almighty Spirit does not interfere, won't interfere until the time is right. I venture to guess that when the spirit world is in jeopardy. The time to intervene will be at hand. All evil will perish. Utopia forever and ever. That is worth waiting for."

Clayton smiled. Hugged the little angel at hearing those words he said, "We waited in joyful bliss until Jason was ready to let go of his physical body and join the spirit world. But Alma and I did not realize what Andrea had planned."

THIRTY-FIVE
Jason's death

Jason had been at the Inn for a month. He had accepted Babs and his new surroundings. He didn't wander by himself, too much hassle pushing the wheelchair, and he didn't want to make new friends.

Babs wanted him to meet someone. On any occasion, she'd tell Jason of a new resident or let him in on the latest gossip. Babs, being a walking tabloid, it amazed Jason how much gossip Babs could rattle off.

One day Jason wheeled himself by the doorway and watched people. Mainly the nurse aides hustled about the hallway. He didn't know his neighbors, which suited him. Nevertheless, this day he sat in the hallway. He noted the door cracked open to the room across the hall. The name tag in the slot indicated a woman resident. Lisa Abernathy. He had never noticed the name. Had life soured him this much?

Jason wheeled the chair to Lisa's door. He gently knocked, "Hello. May I come in?" He didn't hear a response.

He slowly pushed the door wide open so he could wheel himself inside. He saw a bed like the one in his room. A body, hooked up to a feeding tube, barely outlined the covers. He wheeled further into the dimly lit room. A faint scent of lilacs reached his nostrils, like the English gardens he had visited long ago. The darkroom had an aura of somberness.

He came in wide-eyed, astonished at what he gazed at—every inch of wall space covered with cards. Get well cards, birthday cards, Christmas cards, all occasion cards, this had to be a Guinness World Record. He had never seen so many cards in one room. He delicately flipped open an Easter card, signed Dad. He looked at the bed. The body lay quiet, not moving a muscle, whom he ascertained to be Lisa Abernathy. More astonished, the woman looked young. This could be Sage. He stared at her. She even looked like his daughter.

Jason blinked, rubbed his eyes. Sage appeared in the bed, withered. He became horrified, swiftly turned his chair around, pumped the wheels and his feet as fast as he could manage. Jason had to exit the room immediately as he rapidly sped to his room; sharp pains shot through his legs.

Safe in his room, the pain subsided. He grabbed the faded picture of Sage and cried.

Wiping his tears, he placed the picture on his lap. His eyes became heavy with sleep—he let the sleep take over. His body limp slowly faded into dreamland.

Babs knocked on the door and entered as effervescent as ever, arousing Jason. He slowly stretched back into life.

"Jason. Why aren't you out of here? The rooms are drab so you won't spend time here. There are all kinds of activities and stuff to do, like swimming, crafts, gardening, movies or people-watch at the bistro. I'll be glad to take you anywhere. Let's go to the bistro. Maybe you'll meet Mrs. James. She's widowed. She hangs out there around this time. She's funny. You'd like her."

Apathetic, Jason answered, "Thanks, Babs. I like the solitude. I've been alone for such a long time I don't think I have the patience for others or stuff. For most of my life, I've been outgoing. Now, life has caught up. I like solitude. Tell me, Babs, what happened to Lisa Abernathy?"

Babs looked across the hallway at the closed door. "Lisa? A sweet girl. She's in a coma, and I think she's twenty-four. She was in a horrible car accident, barely survived. By the time an emergency team arrived, I think she had died. The paramedics have cardiac monitors, and they hooked her up on the spot and got her going again. She stayed in the hospital for six months—transferred here when life support was removed and breathed independently. Sadly, I've never seen anyone visit her. She receives cards every day, along with lilac scent soaps. I read each one to her. Do you think she hears me? I think she does.

Babs smiled, continued her insistence on entertainment.

"May I bring you a newspaper, a magazine, book? I can bring a movie to your room. We have a great movie library."

"At my age, happiness is being continent," Jason quipped. Babs chuckled.

"Are you hungry?"

"When do we eat?" Jason asked, being cordial.

"Anytime. No schedules, remember? The kitchen is open twenty-four hours a day. May I bring you some fruit? Something to drink?"

"No thanks. I'm fine," Jason slowly answered, trying to forget the image of Lisa Abernathy.

In his far off thoughts, Jason said, "I've had pleasant dreams lately. This place is so restful. I haven't been at peace for a long time. My daughter died at twenty years of age, back in 1996, exactly one month before her twenty-first birthday. Can you imagine that? I've learned to live with it through time, but don't let anyone tell you time heals. That's a bunch of bull. Since her death, I've had a deep sadness. An empty feeling." Jason took a deep breath then continued, "My dreams have been of her. I see her as she was, young, vibrant, and beautiful. She slowly vanishes, and I feel empty but at peace."

"Oh, Jason. It's a dream. Let me take you somewhere."

At last, Jason gave in, "Okay. I used to manipulate a cue stick like a pro at one time. I loved to play billiards, but these old legs won't let me anymore. I haven't been swimming in a while. Let's go swimming."

Babs marked her eagerness by cheers and applauds.

"Ye-ah, Jason! We have a heated pool. You'll have a great time. I know it."

As Babs wheeled Jason back to his room, Jason said, "I enjoyed the swim very much. Thanks for not giving up, Babs. Would you bring me some soup? Anything is fine.

"Good old chicken soup always hits the spot."

"Fine. I'll eat in bed. That way, I'm settled in for the night."

Babs delivers his soup, "When you are through eating, push the snack table aside or press the call light. I'll be here to clean up, okay? Do you want
the TV on?"

"No, I've had all the excitement I can take. I'll work on my soup. That's enough labor for tonight. Thanks. Good night."

Babs slowly walked out, making sure everything was in order.

"Good night Jason."

Two in the morning, June 6, 2016, making her usual rounds, Babs quietly entered Jason's room; the snack table pushed to the side. The night light revealed not much had been eaten. She took the tray out when instinct told her to check on Jason. She turned back, glanced down at him. He appeared too tranquil. She gently took his wrist, feeling for a pulse. Nothing. She felt his neck, feeling for the pulse on the carotid artery. Nothing. She knew. He had let go. Ceremoniously, she made the sign of the cross.

"Rest in peace, Jason. Good-bye."

Babs somberly made her way to the nurses' station to inform them of Jason's death.

THIRTY-SIX
Andrea & Jason

Astonished by the familiar voice, Jason asked, "Andrea? Is Sage here too?"

"Please don't say another word. Before you are true of this world, I must have a trinity."

A doorway opened, in walked Clayton and Alma. They encircled Jason and joined hands, chanting, "Enter the world of the spirit with life everlasting."

Jason opened his eyes. He was in an angelic white room surrounded by familiar faces. He smiled.

"I knew it would be like this. Peace at last! Why didn't I let go ten years ago? That's when my anguish and emptiness intensified like my heart was locked in a monastery, unable to escape. I don't know what kept me going. I moved to a pleasant place, though I had emptiness, I found tranquillity."

Jason stood and hugged his mom and dad. The love he felt miraculous. Reminiscent of the days of his youth, innocent love.

"It's been a long time. I'm glad you are all here to meet me."

Clayton said, "Son, it is wonderful to see you. Please listen. Your mother and I relinquished being your guides. Andrea desperately wants to explain things. Mom and I cannot stay in the physical form. We love you, son. We know you will make the right choice, and join us soon."

Clayton and Alma hugged their son emphatically, leaving a bit of their energy with him. Looking at Andrea, they understood as a doorway opened. Jason saw a bright light take the familiar forms. The doorway closed, Jason gasped in wonderment.

"What is happening? Why were Mom and Dad so vague? Am I going to see Sage? I've waited so long to see her again. Why isn't she here? Am I going to hell? Is that why everyone is so vague?"

Andrea said, "No, you are not going to hell. There is no such place. Before I explain, please touch me. I yearned your touch."

Andrea guided Jason to the center of the catacomb and whispered, "Stand here. I'm going to become energy and engulf your soul. Devoid of all except love, invigorating the depth of our souls."

Jason stood perfectly still. Andrea slowly walked around him. She stopped behind him ever so close; her physical body turned to energetic light, gradually intensifying and slowly flowing through Jason. Their stupendous joining, magical.

Does time matter here? Jason could not tell if a split second or hours passed. Once again behind Jason, Andrea reappeared in physical form. She continued the circle around him—the finale to their last consummation.

"This must be heaven," Jason exclaimed, spellbound.

Facing Jason, looking into his eyes, Andrea said, "I missed you so much. Your being will excite me until the end. Please listen and don't interrupt me until I finish. If you do, I won't last." Pausing, Andrea softly said, "Sage is gone forever."

Upon saying those words, Andrea's energy became dull. Staggering to maintain control, she heard Jason gasp.

"Sh-hh. I'm at fault. She made the wrong choice in life, and her physical body died prematurely. I wanted her to have a second chance. Hoping she would know unconditional love as we did. Alas, things went wrong. I stayed in the physical form too long. I became obsessed with the desire for her to go back. I ignored the wickedness in the physical world. I maintained, if Sage loved Rudy as much as she said, maybe deep inside, he truly loved her too. She expressed her first union as exhilarating and unforgettable. I did not want to remember how first love clouds the mind. She knew lust, not love. If only she had gone with her friends, you and I would be in joyful bliss. Instead."

Andrea could not continue. She sobbed. Her physical presence–slowly fading, her glow, lost its luster. Jason comforted her without a word.

"Jason, I've held on this long only to try to make you understand and to ask for your forgiveness."

Saying those words, Andrea sobbed again; she faded, became frail. She began to meditate. She had to continue.

"Jason. I suppressed rational thinking. Confused by my obsession and Sage's desire, I gave way to forbidden emotions. Irrational thoughts. I realized Sage knew one-sided love, a very destructive love. Rudy was a user. I knew it—I ignored it. Instead, I allowed him to use Sage in both lifetimes. He gratified himself. Nothing else mattered to him. I did not want to send her back to Rudy. It was the only way she would agree to the rebirth. I could only send her back if she agreed to go back. Her choice was Rudy or the oblivion crypt. That's when I should have stopped. I still had enough pure love for both of us. We should have entered the eternal lights; Sage was so innocent. She would have forgotten about Rudy soon enough. Instead, I pushed the limit, willing to give up paradise for Sage to have a second chance, for her to know unconditional love. Maybe if I had never known unconditional love, I wouldn't have been so adamant. I know vividly now there is no second chance for unconditional love. It must be acquired the first time. There is no second chance in the physical world.

Further, clouded by emotional thinking, I remembered giving up everything to be with her. What parent wouldn't do the same? My Sweet Basil, I wanted so much for her. For all that, I ignored Rudy's part. He was the second half of the equation I suppressed. I made my fantasy of a beautiful and blissful second life; I gave up everything as Sage would never know of our existence ever again. Her new parents would be her guide ever after. It was worth it for her to experience the pinnacle of love and fulfillment we knew.

This moment would be different if everything went right, you and I crossing over now. Eternal bliss. Do you suppose I wanted to relive my life?

In all my dark desires and denials, maybe that's why I became so obsessed?

I'm exhausted, Jason. Please forgive me so I can go in peace. I've decided to enter the oblivion crypt, as I do not want to continue, not even in utopia. I want to hear you are at peace with me."

Melancholy Jason stood there, looked up, and then around the entire catacomb. He saw emptiness; he could even feel the void. Andrea, becoming a fading vision.

Jason said, "I hungered for this moment, to see you and Sage. I imagined us happy for all time. The thoughts of an old man also suppressing the cruelties of the physical world. I remember letting go of Sage. It was the most difficult thing I'd ever done. She was too young to die. I wished it had been me. Had I the choice to give her a second chance? I would have done it without hesitation. There is nothing to forgive Andrea. To me, you were an admiration in the physical world. In the spirit world, you are my saint. You've done nothing a loving mother wouldn't do for her child."

Embracing the last of her fading form, Jason tenderly continued, "Please stay. Let's cross the doorway to eternity. We can still have each other."

Meekly Andrea said, "It's too late for me. Sage's memories will always stay within me. My love for her ran too deep. Waiting for you has proven that. Being deprived of her soul, knowing she will be no more, I am hollow. I upset the balance. I knew the risk."

"Can't someone help us? Isn't there someone powerful enough to bring her soul back? Where is God, any God?" Jason asked vehemently.

"Jason. Stop. I am at fault. I pleaded for approbation and sanctioning. I fully knew the consequences."

Quiet for a moment to regain her strength, Andrea explained, "The catacomb is the entrance to paradise or demise of the soul. The trinity or lack of it determines eternity or oblivion. The oblivion crypt is the end of the soul. True death. Eternity is blissful, waiting for the end of greed. End of pain and sorrow. End of death. The Almighty Spirit reigns now. Soon the Perfect Being will command. Until the Perfect Being reigns, the souls may sometimes intercede. I elected to send our Sage back to intervene. Knowing, if it did not turn out, her second physical death would also be the

death of her soul. No one can bring her back. That's the result of interference when things go wrong. Had Rudy been a loving and supportive father, Sage would be in the physical form now. You and I would be together again forever." Andrea's quivering voice spoke the last words, "Farewell, my love.
Forgive me. Find the loving spot to cross over."

Andrea attempted the last touch. She was too weak. The last glow of her essence was her final tribute to Sage and Jason. Andrea's soul vanished.

Alone, Jason touched the spot where Andrea had been, feeling nothing. He sank to the floor, his hands over his face weeping convulsively.

"Jason, my son, How can I squelch your sorrow?" Clayton asked.

"Father. I expected the afterlife to be miraculous and astonishingly beautiful. Instead, I encounter sorrow and real death. Why?"

"Son, I do not know the answer. A lot of reasons led you to this point. You can still cross the gateway to eternity; I will lead you. We must do it now. Staying here much longer will weaken your inner love. Follow me, Son."

Clayton extended his arm. Jason reached up touched his dad's hand.

"Dad. Wait. I know you love me. I can't go."

"Son. Please. Don't make the same mistake Andrea made."

"No, Dad. I can't. Thanks for coming through again. Somehow, our touch just now made me realize, Andrea's touch was special."

"Son, the love of a parent versus the love of a spouse, is different. It should be. There are different types of love, and some can even be deadly. Don't succumb to the deadly love."

"Andrea risked everything. In both worlds. All for unconditional love. We took on the world together; how can I continue? Our love would be in vain." Jake cried out in agony."

"Son. Once you cross over, you will find peace and tranquillity—most of all, real love.

Love from the soul is genuine. Andrea wronged you and Sage. No death is premature. No matter at what age the body dies, in the physical world, once is enough. You and Andrea happened to find each other and knew unconditional love. A little miracle happened with no intercession. That's the way it's supposed to be. No one should interfere; Andrea forgot that or didn't want to remember. Their demise was Andrea's fault. Even in the spirit world, we have choices. Don't abandon paradise. Negative thoughts now surround this catacomb as too many souls have died; that is cataclysmic. Let's leave. Now."

Jason emphatically said, "I have made up my mind. I do not want to exist
in eternity without my Andrea. Least of all without my Sage. Our love transcends beyond the heavens. I do not want to forget that. I can't go on. I won't go on."

Trying to understand, plus help Jason comprehend, Clayton said, "Son. You and Andrea were special people. The reason Andrea could even ask for
approbation–she was a very good person. You and her helped many people. Strangers. How many times did you open the restaurant doors to the hungry? How many donations did you give that came from the heart? Those are the actions that count. Son, there are two kinds of living souls. Good and very good. No one is better; no living soul is above any other. Andrea began getting thoughts of superiority because she stayed in the physical body too long. Her soul had extra energy all along because of her goodness. So do you. As I said, you two were special. No one ever knows how special they are until they let go of the physical body. But the physical body becomes our weakness in the catacomb. We can't stay long in these former selves. Time here depends on the good or the very good of the soul. Our time is almost up. We must leave."

A doorway opened, Clayton stepped across, becoming a bright light. He reached for Jason, trying to pull him through. Stepping back, Jason turned and walked to the spot where Andrea had been.

The entrance closed, the room started to get dark. Jason looked at his form slowly vanishing.

"I forgive you, Andrea," He whispered.

Remembering Andrea's final touch, Jason smiled in contentment as his soul vanished into the oblivion crypt.

THIRTY-SEVEN
Cross Over

Poised, Clayton explained to the little angel. "Anytime souls enter the oblivion crypt, the catacomb needs a benevolent sweep. The risk of any hateful, negative emotions permeating beyond this space is unthinkable. It will not be allowed to happen.

Since Alma and I were part of the trinity, we had to perform the final sweep. We had to enter as perfect positive energy. Our energies going around the entire catacomb leaving only pure love.

We moved around this catacomb, absorbing negativity as our glow started to tarnish. Adverse feelings are strong. Too many souls had died. We quietly finished the sweep of destructive energy, knowing we would never see our beautiful family again.

That disturbed me. I questioned the existence of paradise and the compassion of God."

Clayton bowed his head in shame.

"Paradise did not betray me. God did not betray me. Human desires and human choices did—provoking the death of my family. Sage got stuck in the middle as Andrea's convoluted desires destroyed my innocent granddaughter. As I told Jason, these bodies, in the catacomb become our destruction. The transition is an event that has happened since the beginning of death. This will continue. Whether I choose eternity or the oblivion crypt, this event will continue. The catacombs of the afterlife are beginning to true immortality.

The soul is free to roam peacefully, to experience trueness and oneness with creation. I, too, almost lost paradise."

Warily Clayton rose. The little angel in his protective hold.

"Their choice was destruction, little one. My poor Sage—forsaken, I'll miss you. We have suffered enough. Let's meet Alma. Eternity is better." Clayton had found his peace.

Clayton made his way around the catacomb searched for the entrance, the loving spot. He sang the fifth verse to Amazing Grace as he searched. He slowly came to a stop.

"Here, feel the loving energy, little one. This is where we cross over." The little angel smiled a huge toothless smile.

Clayton touched the spot, a glorious entrance opened. He could feel Alma's soul waiting. Smiling at the little angel in his arms, the joyful baby cooed as they crossed over.

Their physical bodies vanished, turning to pure energy and pure love. Two more loving souls allowed to meld with other eternal souls until called upon to guide.

The entrance faded, leaving all the memories behind in the catacombs of the afterlife.

"This is the second death."
The Revelation 20:14

THE END